THE EDENBOURG TATTLER

April 2001

Word has it that **Rowena Wilde**,
lady-in-waiting to Princess Isabel,
has devoted herself to caring
for the two-year-old son of gorgeous
royal cousin **Jake Stanbury**—
the number-one suspect in King Michael's
disappearance!—while the Americans are
still on Edenbourg soil. However, what
started as a simple "favor" seems
to have escalated into something a bit
more long-term—for Jake has just
proposed marriage to the lovely virgin!
But will a secret Rowena holds in her heart
keep their temporary arrangement from
becoming a lifetime commitment?

Now Nicholas is missing, too!
Or is he?

* * * * * *

Check out next month's
Code Name: Prince
(SR#1516)
by Valerie Parv
to find out what happens!

"Rowena Wilde," Jake released his handful of Luke's

Dear Reader,

The year is off to a wonderful start in Silhouette Romance, and we've got some of our best stories yet for you right here.

Our tremendously successful ROYALLY WED series continues with *The Blacksheep Prince's Bride* by Martha Shields. Our intrepid heroine—a lady-in-waiting for Princess Isabel—will do anything to help rescue the king. Even marry the single dad turned prince! And Judy Christenberry returns to Romance with *Newborn Daddy*. Poor Ryan didn't know what he was missing, until he looked through the nursery window....

Also this month, Teresa Southwick concludes her much-loved series about the Marchetti family in *The Last Marchetti Bachelor*. And popular author Elizabeth August gives us *Slade's Secret Son*. Lisa hadn't planned to tell Slade about their child. But with her life in danger, there's only one man to turn to....

Carla Cassidy's tale of love and adventure is *Lost in His Arms,* while new-to-the-Romance-line Vivienne Wallington proves she's anything but a beginning writer in this powerful story of a man *Claiming His Bride*.

Be sure to come back next month for Valerie Parv's ROYALLY WED title as well as new stories by Sandra Steffen and Myrna Mackenzie. And Patricia Thayer will begin a brand-new series, THE TEXAS BROTHERHOOD.

Happy reading!

Mary-Theresa Hussey

Mary-Theresa Hussey
Senior Editor

Please address questions and book requests to:
Silhouette Reader Service
U.S.: 3010 Walden Ave., P.O. Box 1325, Buffalo, NY 14269
Canadian: P.O. Box 609, Fort Erie, Ont. L2A 5X3

The Blacksheep Prince's Bride

MARTHA SHIELDS

SILHOUETTE *Romance*®

Published by Silhouette Books

America's Publisher of Contemporary Romance

Special thanks and acknowledgment are given to Martha Shields for her contribution to the Royally Wed series.

To Lisa Turner

 SILHOUETTE BOOKS

ISBN 0-373-19510-9

THE BLACKSHEEP PRINCE'S BRIDE

Copyright © 2001 by Harlequin Books S.A.

Visit Silhouette at www.eHarlequin.com

Printed in U.S.A.

Books by Martha Shields

Silhouette Romance

MARTHA SHIELDS

grew up telling stories to her sister in the back seat of the family Rambler on the way to visit their grandparents in Florida. A way to pass the time turned into a love of words, which led to an education in journalism. Fresh out of college, Martha discovered romance novels and finally found a focus for her writing. Martha lives in Memphis, Tennessee, with her husband of over twenty years, a college-age daughter and a Cairn "terror" who can't believe he's not in Kansas anymore. During the day, Martha tries to make college courses sound exciting, and at night, she escapes the pressures of the day by weaving tales of romantic worlds, hoping readers can do the same.

You can keep up with Martha's new releases via her Web site, which can be reached through the author page at www.eHarlequin.com.

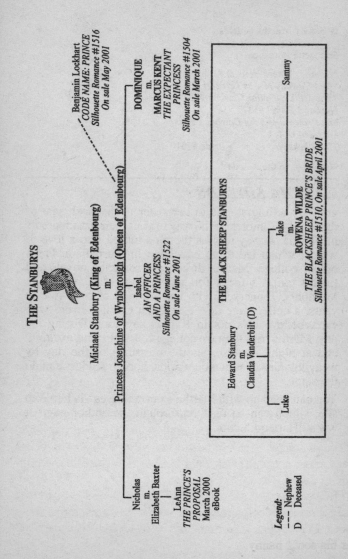

THE STANBURYS

Michael Stanbury (King of Edenbourg)
m.
Princess Josephine of Wynborough (Queen of Edenbourg)

Benjamin Lockhart
CODE NAME: PRINCE
Silhouette Romance #516
On sale May 2001

DOMINIQUE
m.
MARCUS KENT
THE EXPECTANT PRINCESS
Silhouette Romance #1504
On sale March 2001

Isabel
AN OFFICER
AND A PRINCESS
Silhouette Romance #1522
On sale June 2001

Nicholas
m.
Elizabeth Baxter
THE PRINCE'S PROPOSAL
March 2000
eBook

LeAnn

THE BLACK SHEEP STANBURYS

Edward Stanbury
m.
Claudia Vanderbilt (D)

Luke

Jake
m.
ROWENA WILDE
THE BLACKSHEEP PRINCE'S BRIDE
Silhouette Romance #1510, On sale April 2001

Sammy

Legend:
- - - Nephew
D Deceased

Chapter One

Rowena Wilde hated this house.

The Dowager Cottage was a dismal place. Built three centuries ago of native granite, the three-story "cottage" sat on the edge of the cliff like an old woman hunkered down against the storms blowing off the North Sea.

It was where extraneous queens grieved for lost husbands, relived former glory and waited to die.

As she stood with one hand wrapped around a cold iron spoke on the front gate, Rowena recalled the times she'd accompanied Princess Isabel as she visited her grandmother, who'd died three years ago. They'd sipped tea in the gloomy parlor with heavy velvet curtains shutting out the light. Though central heat had been installed years ago, the house was never warm. Even with a blazing fire. Even in the middle of July.

Rowena had known she'd have to stay here when she and Isabel had concocted this plan. Which was one reason she'd been half-hoping Jake Stanbury would refuse to accept her as his son's nanny.

The cottage was full of ghosts, and Rowena had never been comfortable around ghosts.

The other reason, of course, was Jake.

Jake and the Dowager Cottage. Alone, each was a daunting prospect. Together...

Rowena shivered despite the bright April afternoon sunlight.

Both Jake and the cottage got her blood pumping, but for vastly different reasons—all related to fear.

Which was ridiculous.

Taking a deep breath, Rowena marshaled her inner resolve.

There was nothing to be afraid of. The cottage was just a pile of stone. She could dissipate the gloom by tearing down curtains and turning on lamps. And Jake...

Well, she was here for a reason. As long as she kept her mind on her purpose, she wouldn't get sidetracked by feelings she understood all too well...and dreaded.

Rowena forced her lips into her customary smile. Her mother had always said that the best way to conquer fear was to smile your way through it. She'd learned a long time ago that her mother was right. As long as she was smiling, she couldn't scream.

Rowena released the gate latch...wishing she didn't feel like Sleeping Beauty about to prick her finger.

"I'm going to get you."

Jake Stanbury stopped dead, his hand still on the knob of the massive, intricately carved front door. He recognized the voice immediately.

So Rowena Wilde had moved in.

The new nanny's heavily sinister tone seemed to prove the possibility that had occurred to him when his royal cousin, Princess Isabel, had suggested her lady-in-waiting as caregiver for his two-year-old son—the possibility that Rowena had been placed in his household as a spy.

What the hell was he going to do now? Leave her here to poke through his papers and roam the dreary old house he'd been assigned when Sammy's noisy antics became too much for the guests—notably Edward, his own father—in the palace apartment where they'd been staying? What if she rifled through his things while Sammy was around? Would she blithely tell the boy that his father was suspected of kidnapping the King of Edenbourg?

"I'll find you, Sammy-Jammy. You just wait."

Muffled giggling followed her words.

Relief flooded through Jake. They were playing a game.

Shaking his head, he closed the door and placed his briefcase on the chest in the foyer.

This is what the strain of the past month had brought him to—suspecting a sweet, beautiful young woman of playing Mata Hari. Probably the biggest intrigue Rowena had been involved in was finding the laundress responsible for scorching the princess's favorite gown.

Jake stripped off his suit coat and laid it across his briefcase, then followed the happy sounds to the door of the formal parlor, heavily furnished in some Gothic style. Whoever had decorated this house either had eclectic tastes or access to the palace attic, because every room was decorated with a different period of antiques.

Blindfolded, her arms outstretched, Rowena wandered around the large room. Sammy peeked out from under an antique side table on the other side of the couch, one hand over his mouth to stem the tide of his laughter.

Blind Man's Bluff. Such a simple game, but Jake had never thought to play it with his son, who was having such a good time he relieved Jake of any lingering suspicions. Sammy's happiness was all that mattered.

Ever since Sammy's mother had deserted them, his son

had panic attacks every time Jake had to leave him with a sitter. Which was the main reason Jake needed a nanny.

He was determined to give his son a stable home. He'd been forced to use baby-sitters—strangers to Sammy—when he was out of the house, and had rarely managed to get the same one twice. Since Jake couldn't be with Sammy twenty-four hours a day, he hoped having a live-in nanny would add stability to his son's life.

Though he no longer had to work for a living, Jake's expertise in mergers and acquisitions was in high demand. And there were some offers he couldn't refuse. Like the one presented last week—as a consultant to Edenbourg's acting king, his cousin, Nicholas.

The work was just a way to keep him busy. He knew it, and everyone else knew it. The suggestion that his expertise was needed by Nicholas was simply a way to save the royal family the embarrassment of asking him to turn over his passport so he couldn't leave the country and return to America while they investigated any involvement he might have had in the king's disappearance. *His uncle's disappearance.*

Recognizing the frustrating path his thoughts were traveling down, Jake forced his attention back to the playful pair in the parlor.

Sammy's giggling should've led Rowena right to him, of course, but she flailed around comically, running into tables and upsetting lamps and antique knickknacks which she pretended to barely catch in time. Her antics sent Sammy into fresh peals of laughter.

Jake couldn't suppress a smile, though the tenderness melting his heart was all for his son. It definitely wasn't for the petite, auburn-haired beauty bungling around his living room.

The only thing he felt for Rowena was gratitude. He finally had someone he could leave Sammy with—and feel good about it. Someone who'd already proved she could coax his son out of his panic attacks and shyness.

Jake leaned against the doorjamb to watch their antics, but straightened abruptly a moment later. Something was out of place. The only item in the room made during the last century was a shiny steel step stool…directly in Rowena's path.

He didn't have time to wonder what it was doing there. Vaulting over the couch, he launched himself off the side table just in time to catch Rowena as she stumbled into it.

Their combined momentum took them down, but Jake grabbed her waist and twisted so his back hit the floor first, taking her slight weight.

Rowena didn't scream as they fell, just emitted a quick, "Oh!"

She landed flat on top of him, her legs straddling one of his, her nose buried in his chest. "What in the…?"

Because of the antique oriental rug covering the centuries-old oak floor, Jake wasn't in enough pain to keep his body from reacting—especially when Rowena started squirming to free her hands.

Though his mind denied the feelings every time they surfaced, his body knew that he'd been attracted to Rowena since the instant he'd seen her. And now his body reminded his mind of every moment he'd indulged in sensuous fantasies about what his body wanted to do to her small but oh-so-curvaceous body.

He couldn't remember having such a strong reaction to a woman. Ever. Including his ex-wife.

"Daddy's home!"

His son's cry doused enough flames for Jake's mind to regain control.

He grabbed Rowena's hips to keep them still…but it didn't help. Having his hands on her bottom incited his libido just as much. Her curves were soft and warm, as was the sweet scent of roses wafting through his brain.

He could only hope she was too confused to notice what was happening between them.

When Rowena freed a hand and peeled back her blindfold, the instant of surprise lighting her long-lashed, wonderfully expressive, golden hazel eyes held a hint of pleasure. "Mr. Stanbury."

Or was it another trick of his mind?

He couldn't tell, because the pleasure was quickly masked with concern. "Where did you come from? Are you all right?"

Having clambered out from under the table, Sammy threw himself onto the pile.

Jake emitted a soft "oof" with the added weight.

Rowena struggled to rise. "Oh, dear. Sammy, please get off. We're crushing your father."

Jake smiled. "Don't be ridiculous."

Rowena couldn't free herself with Sammy half on top of her. "Allowing you to breathe is ridiculous?"

He chuckled. "The two of you together don't weigh as much as one normal person."

Her dark red-brown eyebrows drew together as if she couldn't decide whether he was insulting or complimenting her. "And just how often do you have 'normal' people on top of you?"

"Often enough to tell," he countered.

"Daddy, guess what?"

"What, Sammy?"

"Ena's here."

"I know." Jake's smile turned to a grin. "Her elbow is sticking into my ribs. Or is that your knee?"

"Why didn't you say something?" She carefully extricated herself from between them.

"I did." Jake sat up easily, bringing Sammy with him. He froze immediately.

Rowena had rolled to her knees and her silk blouse had

pulled away from her chest. Jake had a clear vision of two wonderfully ripe breasts falling into a black silk bra that would've done Victoria's Secret proud.

As he swallowed the thick lump which suddenly stopped his air supply, Sammy scrambled over to Rowena, who sat back Indian-style and patted the full skirt that modestly covered her legs. She smiled fondly and settled Sammy in her lap.

Though Jake felt deserted, he was glad Rowena was covered up, and that she was unaware of how much he wanted to slowly unbutton every silk-covered button and—

"Thank you for rescuing me, Mr. Stanbury. Although there was no need."

Jake's attention swung back to reality with a hard blink. "No need? You were about to break your neck."

"I doubt it would've broken." Her smile turned impish. "As you pointed out, I'm not very tall. Which means my neck is much closer to the ground than yours."

Beautiful, funny and she could turn a joke on herself as well. Jake had always admired people who could laugh at themselves. He'd found it an indication of intelligence and self-confidence beyond the norm.

Damn.

What the hell was he doing sitting on the floor with her? The last thing he needed was to let his libido lead him down the path to destruction. He'd been there, done that.

Annette had taken his heart and ripped it into shreds—which she threw in his face as she walked out the door for a man with more money and more ambition.

And Jake had a sneaking suspicion that Rowena had more than beauty in common with Annette.

His cousin's lady-in-waiting didn't top the list of the hot palace buzz. The gossip was low-key and inconsistent. Still, Jake had made enough firsthand observations and gleaned enough information to piece together an unflattering picture.

Rowena dated more than a few of the diplomats and officials who visited Edenbourg, never going out with the same man more than a few times. But what was more important, she never dated anyone who didn't have a title.

He'd learned too late that Annette had only married him because of his royal blood. Annette had learned too late that she wouldn't benefit from his connections to the royal family of Edenbourg.

He was American through and through, and didn't give a damn about a country he'd never visited, or a family who'd never so much as sent him a birthday card.

Rowena also had a flirtatious nature in common with Annette, which he'd witnessed on the few occasions she'd attended royal functions. She flitted around the palace rooms like a butterfly, bestowing her devastatingly bright, sweetly impish smile on every man there...except him. Because he didn't have a title.

Jake shoved aside the irritation that realization always brought. He was glad she didn't come on to him. It made it easier to listen to his brain rather than his libido. He was definitely not interested in having a relationship with her.

At least, that's what he kept telling himself.

He'd all but panicked when Isabel had suggested Rowena as his nanny. But since the proposal came from his royal cousin, he knew it was yet another offer he couldn't refuse.

He'd been able to avoid close contact with the lovely lady-in-waiting for the month he'd been forced to stay in Edenbourg. And because he knew he couldn't avoid her altogether if they lived in the same house, he'd planned to stay clear of her as much as possible when he was home.

He certainly *hadn't* planned to take a tumble with her on the parlor floor the minute he walked through the door. Or to be sitting here longing to drag her onto his lap. He would snake one arm around her tiny waist, then with the other

he'd stroke back her thick, richly-hued auburn hair and kiss
the soft skin of the small, curving neck——

Damn.

Jake dragged his eyes away from the lovely neck she
joked about. What was wrong with him? Sammy was sitting
right there on her lap.

This was not starting out well.

The smart thing would be to stand up—now—dust himself
off and make some excuse about paperwork.

Instead, he said, ''Jake.''

''Pardon me?''

If he could've kicked himself in his traitorous mouth, he
would've. His insistence on her calling him Jake had come
in a moment of weakness…right after he'd agreed to accept
her as Sammy's nanny.

He'd had to take Sammy along with him to the palace one
day when the sitter didn't show. Isabel had simply nodded
to Rowena, who stepped forward and charmed Sammy so
much he allowed her to lead him away, all smiles. And his
son had returned the same way. Right then, he'd known Rowena was worth her weight in platinum and he'd offered her
the nanny job on the spot.

That was his excuse at the time. What was it now?

But…he had to finish what his mouth started. Didn't he?

''When you agreed to stay here with Sammy, you also
agreed to call me Jake, not Mr. Stanbury. We shook hands
on it, remember?''

''Oh. That's right.'' The faintest blush touched her cheek,
and she forced a smile. ''I'm sorry…Jake. I just… I guess
I didn't want to seem forward.''

Her blush caught and held Jake's attention. He'd never
seen Annette blush. His ex-wife was so calculating that she
was no longer capable of blushing.

Damn. Why did Rowena have to go and do that?

There'd been enough of these seemingly insignificant

clues to keep him guessing. To keep him from believing—deep down—the conclusions he'd come to about Rowena. To keep him thinking that there was more to her than she wanted anyone to see.

Jake wanted to peel back the layers and search for the real woman beneath.

Unsettled by the revealing realization, Jake didn't even try to keep sarcasm from his voice. "And you're never forward, are you, Miss Wilde?"

Her face registered mild shock at his rude comment. She started to say something, then pressed her lips together and used them to place a kiss on Sammy's head. From that position, she said softly, "If I have to call you Jake, then you should call me Rowena."

Jake was too much a lawyer to be dragged from the subject so easily. "I—"

Suddenly a bright ray of light struck Jake's eye, catching his attention. Glancing around, he saw afternoon sunlight streaming into the west-facing bank of windows, lighting up the room.

Then he saw why. The heavy velvet curtains had been taken down, though one at each window had been draped on the curtain rod as a swag. Not enough to get in the way, just enough to add a decorative touch.

"I hope you don't mind," she said, a bit defensively. "I couldn't bear to live here in all the gloom."

"Gwoom?" Sammy lifted his head to look straight up at her. "Whatsat?"

She peered down at him. "Remember how dark the room was before you helped me? Gloomy is just another word for that."

"We do all rooms, right? You said?"

Rowena smoothed Sammy's hair off his face, then glanced up at Jake. "If your father doesn't mind."

Jake let go of his pique. Rowena's ambitions were no

concern of his. "I guess that explains what the step stool is doing here. Yes, please take down as many curtains as you like. This is much better. I didn't like it being so dark, either, but I didn't realize I could do anything about it."

She lifted a slender shoulder. "No one has lived here for three years. Every dowager queen redecorates when she moves in, anyway. I'm just saving Queen Josephine the trouble of—"

"What's wrong?" Jake asked when she broke off suddenly.

Her eyes were wide as they met his. "I'm talking as if she'd be moving in soon. Which means I must think, deep down, that…"

"That my uncle is dead."

She nodded fearfully.

Jake was touched by the tears in her eyes. Her emotion was sincere. He'd bet his next consulting fee on it. She really loved his uncle.

He wanted to lean forward and place a comforting hand on the arm wrapped around his son, but didn't. "It's frustrating to everyone, not knowing. I never met my uncle, but from what I've heard, he's a good man."

She searched his eyes, then asked, "You think he's alive?"

Jake didn't look away. "I don't know. If he wasn't, I think they would've found…some evidence."

"You mean his—" Her gaze dropped to Sammy, then she sighed. "I'm sorry. I didn't mean to—"

"He's okay," Jake said. "I know you're worried. I'm worried, too. Everyone's worried."

Their gazes met again, and held. Hers asked questions her lips wouldn't.

Had he kidnapped…and killed…King Michael?

It was the first intimation that she might think so, and once again the possibility flitted across his mind that Rowena had been placed in his house to spy.

Jake wasn't the only suspect, of course. His cousin, Nicholas, Jake's father, Edward, and his older brother, Luke, were also considered to have motivation since they were first, second and third in line for the throne, respectively.

Jake was fourth in line, but because he'd been the first to see the smashed railing where the King's car had skidded off a cliff and plummeted to the rocky beach below, he was at the top of the list of suspects. He'd called the police, which made him the first on the scene, and automatically made the odds on him rise considerably. At least in the eyes of the authorities.

He supposed he should be flattered that they considered him capable of such a momentous crime—which required significant finesse and forethought—all with a two-year-old in tow after barely having stepped off the plane.

But somehow, he wasn't.

He believed the fabled Chamber of Riches—reputed to hold a king's ransom in royal jewels—was just that…a fable. Obtaining the key to the Chamber was supposedly his motive.

Living here, Rowena would have ample opportunity to find any evidence linking him to his uncle's disappearance, which had happened on the day Jake had landed in Edenbourg.

There wasn't any evidence to find, of course, but they didn't know that…yet.

The thought of Rowena going through his things while he was away made him want to open the front door and toss her straight out into the royal rose bushes.

Then he realized that wasn't what he wanted to do at all. What he really wanted to do was convince her of his innocence. He wanted her to believe in him, to believe he wasn't capable of killing anyone, much less his uncle. Even one he'd never met.

Damn. This definitely was *not* starting out well.

Rowena was the first to look away. "What time would you like dinner?"

Her question startled him. "You're going to cook?"

She nodded. "Mrs. Hanson left as soon as I arrived this afternoon. I think she was a bit miffed that you left Sammy with her."

A spy who cooked? That was unique…unless she was planning to poison him. But he didn't think she was here to do away with him, just to see what he knew about the king's disappearance.

"I know she was upset with me, but I didn't arrange for yet another baby-sitter because I thought you'd be moved in by noon."

"I'm sorry. Something came up with Isabel."

"I understand."

Jake pressed a thumb into his temple. The strain really was getting to him. Rowena was no spy. She was a lady-in-waiting, a glorified maid who happened to be very good with children. She was here as a nanny, not a spy.

That was why they had him up at the palace the best part of every day. So the ones who were qualified could watch him in the comfort of their own home.

"You don't have to cook. Why don't you go get yours and Sammy's things and we'll go to a restaurant. Know a good one?"

She stared at him as if he'd turned blue. "You want me to come with you?"

"You don't want to?"

"It's not that. It's just… Why?"

Her amazement surprised him. Surely she'd gone to fancy restaurants on all her high-powered dates. "I don't know. Because you're hungry?"

She cocked her face and peered at him sideways. "I'd rather cook, if it's all the same to you."

"Fine. I just wanted to save you the trouble. You've been with Sammy all afternoon, and I know how exhausting that can be." He butted Sammy's knee with a fist. "No offense, little guy."

Sammy giggled.

"I'm fine," Rowena insisted. "And don't worry. I won't poison you. I cooked all my father's meals after my mother died when I was twelve. I'm quite a good cook."

"I didn't think..." He glanced away guilty. The thought *had* occurred to him. "Never mind."

Her words relieved the last vestiges of suspicion, and Jake's stomach chose that moment to grumble about not eating since breakfast.

Rowena chuckled, and finally relaxed. "It's not your mind that's complaining."

"You really don't have to cook, you know."

"Tell that to your stomach." With a hand on Sammy's bottom, she pushed him to his feet. "Sammy and I laid out everything in the kitchen. It will only take half an hour."

Since she was determined, Jake rose and held out a hand.

She paused with both hands on the floor, glanced at his hand, then up at him.

"It won't poison you," he said softly.

She didn't retort, or even smile. After a noticeable hesitation, she gingerly placed her hand in his.

Jake wrapped his long fingers around her slender hand and pulled her to her feet. Her weight was so slight and he was feeling so unnerved, he miscalculated and pulled with enough force to yank her against him.

"Oh," they said in unison.

She lifted her head, then they both went still.

Her startled golden gaze mesmerized him, narrowing his awareness to the space around them. Her lips could be featured in an ad for collagen injections. They were lusciously moist and slightly parted in surprise. Her breathing was shallow and rapid.

She trembled ever so slightly in his arms. With fear? Desire? Both?

Jake could feel her left fist digging into his chest. Her right hand was still captured in his left. Her slight weight leaned into him, one leg braced between his.

He wanted to do far more than kiss her, and the feeling jarred him back to reality.

He couldn't touch her. She was too much like Annette.

She stepped back a second before he let her go.

Without glancing up, she murmured, "Sorry. I'll...I'll... Oh yes. I'll go prepare dinner."

He watched as she fled the room.

Her discomfiture told him two things. She was attracted to him as well, and she was fighting it just as hard.

The only reason for that he could come up with was that he didn't have a title.

"Daddy, play with me."

Jake turned his attention to his son, convinced he'd done the right thing.

Rowena knocked softly, then pushed open the door between the dining room and the parlor with the intention of telling Jake and Sammy their dinner was ready.

Instead, she hesitated.

Father and son were sitting together in a burgundy damask wingback chair by a window open to let in a soft spring breeze and the sound of the surf below. The last rays of the sun caught the side of Jake's face, making the strong lines seem even more angular.

Jake's long legs were stretched out on an ottoman as he concentrated on a stack of papers in his lap. He'd rolled up his shirtsleeves and tucked his son into the crook of his left arm.

Sammy's little legs barely reached the end of the chair cushion. His attention was riveted on a book laid open across his own lap. He turned the pages slowly and carefully.

Rowena's face relaxed into a smile. What a heartwarming picture they made. A loving father and an adoring son.

How could such a man have kidnapped the king? His very own uncle? Family seemed important to Jake. She'd never seen a father as attentive as he was to Sammy. And though his overtures were hesitant, he took every opportunity to spend time with his newfound cousins.

Was that all for show?

Rowena shook away the tender feelings.

Jake was a suspect in the king's disappearance. That's what she had to concentrate on—trying to find evidence that would incriminate him, which would exonerate Isabel's brother, Nicholas.

Rowena had promised Isabel she'd search high and low for evidence…but now that she was here, she found it difficult to believe Jake capable of such a crime—which meant she had to concentrate doubly hard on her purpose in being here.

Even if she hadn't already known, the incident earlier had proven she was strongly attracted to Jake. She'd almost pushed up on her toes and kissed the man…right there in front of Sammy.

Her stupid attraction was the reason she didn't believe he was guilty. She didn't *want* to believe it. That, and the unhappy realization that finding Jake guilty—a man who loved his son so much—would leave Sammy fatherless.

Concentrating wasn't going to be easy. When she'd felt his obvious reaction to her lying on top of him, all she could think of was wiggling her way up his body and planting her lips on his. Thank God he'd held her in place. Though she'd enjoyed the intimacy of his hands on her derriere, the caress had distracted her long enough for her to pull her wits together and stop.

Who knows what would've happened if he hadn't?

He wanted her. That was plain enough. After he'd pulled her to her feet, he'd almost kissed her. She was as certain of that as she was of her name.

But he didn't *want* to want her—and his sarcastic question had told her why.

You're never forward, are you, Miss Wilde?

He didn't trust her because of her reputation.

Rowena's nails dug into her palms.

How long would Prince Heinrich's duplicity haunt her?

She'd given her heart to the royal rake from Leuvendan five years ago. He'd visited often back then, wooing her passionately. But when she wouldn't sleep with him, he became angry and told everyone that she had anyway, giving them ugly, nasty details from his sick imagination.

That incident, it seemed, had branded her for life. Edenbourg—especially the palace—was a small place. Everyone knew everyone else's secrets...and never forgot.

Many men who came to Edenbourg wanted to date her—either despite her reputation or because of it. She went out with some of them, mostly to keep Isabel happy. But she never slept with a single one—partly to prove she was not the wanton everyone thought her, partly because she just didn't want to.

However, her celibacy didn't help. A few of the men were too honorable to talk about their relationship, but most were too egocentric to let everyone think the woman who slept with everyone else wouldn't sleep with them.

She couldn't win.

Although...

In this situation, perhaps her undeserved reputation would protect her. She was far too attracted to Jake. Though good fathers weren't often rakes, he was still royal. At least, close enough to count.

She'd promised herself that she'd never fall in love again…but especially not with a royal, or any man with a title. They were too self-absorbed, too accustomed to getting their own way.

So, let him believe she was "forward."

As for her, she had to focus on the task she had to perform for her country, for Isabel.

It didn't matter that the task came with shoulders as wide as the horizon, sky-blue eyes capable of peering all the way into her soul, and chiseled lips that demanded, "Kiss me."

Those lips might also be capable of saying, "Kill him," to some thug as he looked a king straight in the eye.

Rowena shivered.

She hated this house. It was always cold.

Chapter Two

Later that evening, Jake held Sammy's door open for Rowena. She tiptoed out and waited for him to close it softly.

He turned and looked down at her in the dim light of the hallway. Though they hadn't been in the same room since dinner, he'd felt her presence in the house all evening. A subtle awareness, a whiff of her lingering scent, a trill of laughter from another end of the house.

He was aware of her now, intensely, as he'd been while they'd put Sammy to bed.

"Goodnight, Mr. Stanbury," she said with a nervous smile, then turned to leave.

"It's only eight-thirty," he said quickly, reluctant to let her go. "Surely you're not turning in so early?"

She lifted a slender shoulder. "I have a book in my room."

He waved a hand toward the stairs. "I'm going to work in the library. You're welcome to read down there."

She glanced toward the stairs, then back at him. Her eyes zeroed in on his lips, as if she were remembering the kiss they'd almost shared that afternoon.

He hadn't been able to think about anything else all evening. And if she came with him to the library, he wouldn't be able to concentrate on his work.

Why had he asked her?

Because he didn't want to concentrate on his work. The zing in his blood, put there by the presence of this small woman, was infinitely more interesting than international trade briefs.

"No, I shouldn't." Her words sounded breathless.

He should just let her go, but he couldn't. "Why not?"

She seemed surprised that he pushed it. "It's just not a good idea."

Let it go, Jake. Let her go. "Why not?"

She frowned at him. "Because you're a prince and I'm a servant. That kind of…fraternization is frowned upon."

"Perhaps a hundred years ago, but not today."

"We don't do things here the way you do in the United States. Here, we treat our royalty like royalty." She squared her shoulders. "Besides, I want to concentrate on my book. I think I've guessed who the murderer is and he's about to be revealed. So goodnight, Mr. Stanbury. Have a pleasant evening."

She spun on her heel and walked down the hall to the next room, which was now hers. He watched her every stiff step of the way.

Just as she opened the door, he said, "It's Jake, Rowena. Remember that."

At his words, she hesitated just long enough for him to know she had to make herself go into her room.

When her door closed with a loud click, he headed down the stairs.

"Daddy! Guess what?"

Rowena glanced over her shoulder as she reached for the coffeepot…and caught her breath.

Tousled and unshaven, Jake stood in the kitchen doorway, staring at her blankly. "Oh. Rowena. I forgot…I heard noise down here and thought Sammy was trying to make breakfast himself. Mrs. Hanson only cooks lunch and dinner."

He was dressed only in pajama bottoms. Since they weren't rumpled, Rowena knew that he'd thrown them on to rush downstairs…which meant he slept in the nude.

She swallowed with difficulty. That was a little too much information for her comfort zone.

Her gaze wandered over the light mat of dark hair covering his broad, well-defined chest. "I…" She had to swallow to open her suddenly constricted throat. "I know."

The only place she'd ever seen such a beautiful body on a man was in the pages of fashion magazines. Edenbourg's rocky beaches were not exactly a mecca for sunbathers.

"Guess what, Daddy?" Sammy held up his plate. "Ena made me waffles. Booberry."

"She did?" Jake frowned at his son, who had syrup all over his hands and mouth, then glanced up. "I usually fix breakfast."

"I know." Rowena couldn't manage a more coherent answer. She could barely manage to breathe.

Though his eyes were slightly red and his hair hadn't been combed, Jake was the sexiest man she'd ever seen. Or was it *because* of his dishabille that he was sexy?

"Nothing this fancy, though. These look good." Jake picked a bite of waffle from his son's plate. "Oh yeah. These are great."

"I know."

"I usually just fix toast or something."

Jake licked the syrup from his fingers, and Rowena couldn't stop her eyes from following the movements. Her hands clenched, and she wondered what would it feel like to lick the sweetness off those long fingers herself. "I know."

"Or fry up some toad tongues."

"I—"

"Ewwww, Daddy!"

Rowena's attention snapped back into place like a stretched rubber band…with the same sharp sting.

Jake leaned over Sammy, looking at her with one eyebrow lifted.

What was wrong with her? Never in her life had she had a thought like that. Lick syrup off a man's fingers? What was she thinking?

The worst part was—Jake's smile said he knew exactly what she'd been thinking.

Damn.

"Or lizards' gizzards."

Sammy giggled. "You do not!"

"Or—"

"I get it." Rowena fought the urge to touch her blazing cheeks. She'd been caught staring. She'd been around the palace long enough to know how rude—not to mention how dangerous—staring at a man was. She could either apologize or change the subject. "Would you like some coffee?"

"Coffee?" He grinned knowingly, but took her bait. "Sure. Does it come with a waffle?"

She relaxed. "If you like. Plain or—"

"Any more *boo*berries?"

Rowena smiled. She could certainly see where Sammy got his sense of fun. "If you like. But I have to warn you, they're not fresh this time of year. They're frozen."

"Doesn't matter to me. They taste good in the waffles."

She smiled as she poured him a cup of coffee, pleased by his compliment. "How many would you like?"

"Is two too many?"

"For a growing boy like you? I don't think so."

"Growing boy?" Sammy asked. "Daddy?"

Jake tousled his son's hair and began pulling out a chair to sit down. "With many breakfasts like this, I'll be doing plenty of growing...sideways."

Rowena cleared her throat. "Two waffles will take me just long enough for you to shower and put on some clothes." She placed the coffee in his hands. "You can take this with you."

"Black?" He glanced up from the mug. "I like my coffee sweet." He grinned. "Just like I like my—"

She cut him off. "Sugar is on the table. There's cream in the icebox."

"—waffles."

Her eyes narrowed. What was he doing? Flirting with her? And what had last night been about? Read with him in the library? Sharing the space like a married couple?

"I'm sticky," Sammy announced, drawing both their attention. "I'm gonna wash."

Rowena pushed away from the counter. "I'll come with—"

"No, Ena." He paused at the door, placing his sticky hand on the jamb. "I'm a big boy. I do it."

She watched her charge desert her.

"His third birthday is still three months away," Jake said. "So he's just beginning to make it out of the terrible twos. He's as stubborn as..." He grinned, "...his dad."

Uneasy alone with Jake, Rowena picked up a washcloth and walked over to wipe the syrup off the doorjamb.

Jake turned toward the icebox. "I'm sorry if I shocked you. I just couldn't resist teasing. You seemed so surprised to discover that I have a chest."

So he was teasing, not flirting. Thank God.

"I was...a little," she admitted, but wouldn't admit to herself even a trace of disappointment. "Men don't wander around the palace half-naked, as a rule. Especially not the royals."

Jake pulled open the door of the icebox—it had probably been bought when they still called them that—and reached inside for the cream. "How long have you worked there?"

"Since I was nineteen. Seven years."

He poured a heavy dose of cream into his coffee. "Have you worked for Isabel the whole time?"

Rowena nodded. "I dreamed of working in the palace since I was little. Isabel needed a lady-in-waiting when she turned twenty-one, and my father knew someone on the palace staff who got me an interview. We clicked immediately, and I've been with her ever since."

He heaped three teaspoons of sugar in his coffee and stirred thoughtfully. Without glancing up, he asked, "Any…fringe benefits?"

"Like what? Insurance? Paid vacations?"

His eyes were narrow when he looked up. He stared at her for a long moment, then shook his head. "Never mind. Do you like the job?"

"Of course I do. Isabel has become a good friend."

"Then why are you here?"

Rowena walked back to the sink to rinse out the dishcloth. She'd known this question was coming and had a ready answer. "I'm here because Sammy needs someone to take care of him. Someone who's around more than the occasional sitter. Isn't that why you asked for a nanny?"

"Yes…but why you?"

"There is a distinct shortage of qualified nannies in Edenbourg. Even baby-sitters, for that matter. Our unemployment rate is so low that our daycare workers are paid much higher than those in the States."

"And just what are your qualifications?"

"You didn't ask Isabel when she suggested to you that I come?"

"Answer the question, please."

"Yes, Mr. Barrister." She raised a brow to let him know she recognized his arrogance. "I worked in child care during secondary school. And..." she shrugged "...children seem to like me."

"Sammy certainly does. I'm amazed at how much you've brought him out already."

"Then why are you worried?"

Jake shrugged and took a sip of coffee. "I'm his father. It's my job."

She sighed. "I'm here because I like children. I really do like Sammy. And Isabel asked me to help, since you might be here a while. I'd do anything for her. She's as dear to me as a sister."

"I might be here a while." Jake pounced on her offhand comment. "Why? Because I'm guilty?"

Rowena could've kicked herself. "Guilty of what?"

"Of kidnapping the king."

The lawyer in Jake was definitely showing. Blunt, and to the point. "Did I say that?"

"Do you think it?"

She studied him across the oak table, and decided she could be just as blunt. "Are you?"

"No," came the quick reply.

Rowena was amazed. Not because he denied it, because she believed him. "Then you don't have anything to worry about, do you?"

"I'm not a citizen of this country, and evidence can be manufactured."

She waved his concern away. "Edenbourg is not a third-world country ruled by a despot. We may have dungeons in our castles, but they haven't been used in at least a hundred years."

"But you—"

"I was told you're working with Prince Nicholas on the

revised trade agreement with the European Union, and that's why you'll be here a while.''

He did not look convinced. ''You and I both know—''

''All clean.'' Sammy held up his hands as he appeared in the doorway.

Rowena brightened with more relief than pride in Sammy's accomplishment. ''Great job. Want to help me fix your papa's waffles?''

''Oh boy! I mash booberries, 'kay?''

Rowena dragged the step stool so Sammy could reach the counter. ''Well, we don't mash them. But you can pick out the best ones.''

The next time she glanced toward the door, Jake was gone.

Two days later, Jake settled back against the stone railing of the terrace overlooking the palace gardens and crossed his arms over his chest. He adopted this body language a lot, he'd noticed, when he was in the company of his father and brother.

He usually made a conscious effort to uncross everything, but within a few moments, something else was crossed.

''Jake, you're not listening,'' Edward Stanbury said.

Jake stifled a sigh. His father was as bad as his two-year-old, wanting attention focused on him at all times. The only problem was, his father was fifty-five. ''Yes, I am. You're agreeing with Luke that we shouldn't support Nicholas's position on the immigration clause.''

''You let a foreign underclass in,'' Luke sniffed, ''and you open yourself to all kinds of criminal activity.''

''That's not necessarily true. Meanwhile, with an economy as strong as Edenbourg's, menial jobs go begging for workers.''

''Yes, but what happens when the economy weakens?''

his father argued. "Once you let these people in, it's harder than hell to boot them out again."

"And if you don't have jobs to give them, you have to support them." Luke lit a cigarette and blew the smoke in Jake's face. "They're a liability any way you look at it."

Jake didn't flinch against his brother's stream of smoke. He'd learned a long time ago it was best not to let Luke know he was getting under his skin. "They're *not* always a liability. Having a full workforce will strengthen the economy, so it doesn't get weak. Right now, Edenbourg is begging for workers in the lower-paying jobs. It's worse here than in the States because, as a rule, Edenbourg citizens have a higher level of education."

"You always were soft on…" Luke's attention focused on something behind Jake. He whistled lecherously. "Now there's something that's not a liability…in any country."

It had to be a sexy woman. Jake glanced over his shoulder. His brother was too predictable.

A woman was bent over a child at the edge of the small pond about a hundred yards away, giving them a view of a well-rounded rear end.

"Damn, they grow 'em right over here, don't they?" Luke tossed down his cigarette. "I think I should go show that sweet young thing just how friendly Americans can be."

The woman straightened then, and the sun glinted off deep red highlights in her dark hair.

Rowena.

Jake grabbed his brother's arm. "That's Sammy with his new nanny."

"Well, I'll be…" For once, Luke didn't finish his vulgarity. "No wonder you've been antsy to go home the last couple of nights."

"Isn't that Princess Isabel's lady-in-waiting?" Edward asked. "What's her name?"

"Rowena Wilde." Jake released his handful of Luke's

pinpoint cotton shirt. "And the reason I go home at night is to spend time with my son."

"Yeah, right." Luke grinned. "So when are you going to invite your father and brother home for supper? Is she a good cook, as well?"

"As a matter of fact, she—" Suddenly, Jake stiffened.

Rowena and Sammy were disappearing around the end of the pond, heading for an arbor swing on the other side. From his vantage point above the gardens, Jake could see something Rowena couldn't.

Hidden by a hedgerow and running straight toward them was an enormous mastiff.

"What's wrong?" Edward asked.

"Sammy's afraid of dogs."

Jake bolted down the terrace and took the endless layers of stone steps three at a time. Heart pounding in dread, he vaulted over rose bushes and blasted through a hedge. Still, it took several minutes for him to reach the pond.

When he did, what he saw was so far from the bloody, screaming carnage he expected to see, he skidded to a halt.

Rowena knelt on the ground next to Sammy. The dog sat facing them, tongue lolling, his huge paw lifted and placed in Sammy's hand by Rowena.

His little boy, who'd always been terrified of dogs of any size, was giggling. Actually giggling.

As Jake gaped, Rowena lifted her gaze and her beautiful smile widened. "There's your papa."

Sammy dropped the dog's paw as he turned. "Daddy, guess what? See my doggie? His name's Boo-Boo."

Finally able to move, Jake walked over and knelt beside his son. He casually patted the dog's head. "Yes, indeed, Sammy. I do see the dog. Boo-Boo is a very nice dog."

"His name is Booten Sebastian Cabot the Fourth," Rowena said with a laugh in her lilting voice. "But that's a bit much for a little mouth."

Sammy mimicked his father by stroking Boo-Boo's head. "Good doggie."

"How did you manage this?" Jake couldn't keep the amazement from his voice. "Sammy's always been...a bit leery of dogs."

"This brave little man?" She gave Sammy a hug. "He just needed to see how much dogs are like we are. All they want is a little love."

Boo-Boo butted her arm with his nose.

Rowena laughed and scratched the dog behind his ears. "All right, a lot of love. Isn't that right, you big old baby?"

"Big baby!" Sammy cried, laughing. "Isn't he, Daddy?"

Jake scratched the dog's deep chest. "He sure is."

Boo-Boo gave a little howl, loving all the attention.

Sammy giggled and helped Jake scratch the mastiff's chest. "Can Boo-Boo go to our house?"

"Not today, Sammy," Jake said. "But I'm sure you can visit Boo-Boo any time."

"Of course he can." Rowena stood and held onto the dog's collar. "As a matter of fact, my father's cairn just had a litter of puppies. Is it all right if I take Sammy to see them tomorrow?"

Jake stood, too, and picked Sammy up. "Where does your father live?"

"In a village called Kempten. It's about half an hour's drive."

"You drive?"

"Of course I drive. I can take a car from the palace garage any time." She placed a hand over her brow to shade her eyes from the early afternoon sun as she looked up at him. "Would you like to go with us?"

As he gazed down at her lovely, upturned face, Jake realized he very much wanted to go.

During the past couple of days, he'd discovered that he liked Rowena's method of handling children. Laughter mixed with positive comments rather than frowns and criticism. And she'd just performed a miracle with Sammy.

He wanted to see the man who'd raised her. She must be very loved, to have so much love to give.

To children, of course.

"It would do you good, to get out of the palace for a while," she said. "Have you seen much of Edenbourg?"

"Just the road from the airport to Old Stanbury."

Her forehead wrinkled. "You're the one who found the king's car, aren't you?"

Jake stiffened. "Yes. Why?"

"It's just that the coastline road is not the shortest route from the airport to here."

Jake frowned. Luke had provided him with directions from the airport.

"Are the puppies like Boo-Boo?" Sammy asked.

Rowena smiled. "No, they're a lot smaller. Papa has a Cairn terrier. He bought her when he and I went to Scotland on vacation several years ago."

Jake let go of what was bothering him about the airport road. "Cairn?"

"Ever seen the *Wizard of Oz?*" Rowena asked.

"Who hasn't?"

"Toto was a cairn."

"Toto!" Sammy cried.

"Have you seen the *Wizard of Oz,* Sammy?"

Jake nodded. "We watched part of it a couple of months ago. Until the witch got a little too much for...um...me to take."

Laughter brightened Rowena's dark golden eyes. "She scares me, too."

"Me, too," Sammy admitted.

"Are you going in to the palace?" Jake asked, turning to let her precede him.

Rowena still held onto the dog's collar. "I need to take Boo-Boo back to the kennel."

Sammy struggled against Jake's hold. "I wanna go with Ena."

Jake held on with difficulty. Sometimes holding on to his son was like trying to hold on to an eel in a vat of oil. "I don't know, Sammy."

Rowena met Jake's gaze with an "I agree with you" nod. "Tell you what, Sammy. Go with your papa. I'll be back in just a minute, and I'll take you to see the pool inside the palace. It was built a hundred and fifty years ago."

Sammy was clearly torn, but reluctantly agreed. "'Kay, Ena."

Before there could be any more discussion, Jake turned toward the palace.

Sammy watched Rowena over Jake's shoulder. "Guess what, Daddy?"

"What, Sammy?"

"We go see her puppies tomorrow, right?"

Jake gave his son a hug. "Right, Sammy. Tomorrow we'll go see her daddy's puppies."

Sammy slipped his arm around Jake's neck. "You, too. Right, Daddy?"

"Yes, Sammy. Me, too."

With a contented sigh, Sammy laid his head on Jake's shoulder.

Jake's heart turned over. He didn't care what was going on in the negotiations tomorrow, he was going to see Rowena's puppies.

With Sammy, of course. Just for Sammy.

Chapter Three

As they rounded a mountain curve the next morning several miles outside Edenbourg's capital city of Old Stanbury, Jake settled back into the passenger seat of the Mercedes sedan marked with royal license plates.

"Finally," Rowena muttered from behind the wheel.

"Finally what?"

"You've been sitting on the edge of your seat since we left the palace. Not an easy thing to do with a seat belt on."

"Sorry."

"Did you think I was going to kill us all?"

Actually, he hadn't given her driving a thought, though he'd offered to take the wheel before they left the garage on the way to her father's village of Kempton. The reason he'd finally relaxed was he just felt the chains break that had held him in the palace.

Now that she mentioned it, though, her driving was excellent.

"You're a better driver than I thought you'd be."

"Why would you think I wouldn't be a good driver?"

He shrugged. "How often do you drive? You seem to be stuck in the palace as much as I am, and probably you have a driver if you go somewhere with the princess."

She threw a sharp glance his way. "I haven't gone out much lately, it's true. Things have been hectic since the king disappeared. Isabel has needed me more than usual. But in normal times, I drive to see my father at least once a week."

"You don't even own a car."

"You Americans." Rowena smiled as she navigated a hairpin curve that overlooked a view of an impossibly green valley with a quaint village crawling up the side of a rocky mountain. "Can't survive without at least one vehicle in the garage. Why should I give myself the expense of a car when I can check one out of the royal garage any time? You could, too, you know. You're not a prisoner. You could borrow a palace car and take Sammy anywhere."

"Anywhere on the island, you mean." He didn't mean to sound bitter.

"Well, if I do say so myself, Edenbourg is a beautiful country. We have many sites of interest, whether you like history or nature or the arts...."

"Anything a two-year-old might be interested in?"

"Sammy's almost three, isn't he?"

"Yes, in three months."

"He certainly speaks well for his age."

"I know. He started talking around ten months. Partly, I think, because he had to verbalize his needs." He glanced in the back. Sammy wasn't paying any attention to them. "Annette wasn't the most...attentive of mothers."

"That's so— Oh, look. Here's something that will interest a two-year-old." She slowed the car. "Sammy, look. See the deer? That's a red doe. And look! She has two spotted babies."

"Where?" Sammy craned his neck from his car seat behind them. Rowena had procured one tall enough for Sammy to see out of the windows easily.

"There, through the trees."

"I see them!" Sammy cried. "Can I pet baby deers?"

"Sorry, Sammy." Rowena smiled over her shoulder. "They're not like Boo-Boo. They're wild. If you tried to get close to them, they'd run away."

"Are they scared of me?"

"Yes, they are."

"They think I hurt them?"

"Yes, like you used to run away because you thought dogs would hurt you. They don't know that all you want to do is love them. Oh. There they go."

"Where?" Sammy asked.

"I don't know. Maybe they went home to see their papa." Rowena eased on the accelerator.

Seconds later, Sammy said, "Ena, guess what?"

"Yes, Sammy?"

"I'm not afraid of dogs."

"I know you're not." She beamed at him in the rearview mirror. "Why?"

"'Cause all they wanna do is love me."

"You're such a brave boy, Sammy. I'm proud of you. And your papa is proud of you, too. Aren't you, Jake?"

Jake twisted so his son could see the pride in his eyes. "I'm very proud of you, Sammy. And I love you very much."

"I know, Daddy."

As he turned back around, Jake's attention was caught by Rowena's profile. For such a small woman, she had a strong face…and a strong mind to match.

She glanced over and caught him staring. "What?"

"You should be a child psychologist…or a mother."

A flinch passed over her face so quickly, he couldn't be sure it wasn't a shadow thrown by a tree they passed.

"I don't think so," she said.

"You don't think...which one?"

"Either."

"You don't want children? I can't believe that. You're such a wonderful mother to kids who aren't even your own...and you seem to love them."

"I do love children. They still believe that wonderful, magical things can happen."

"Like Santa Claus and the Easter Bunny?"

"Yes."

"But you don't want children of your own "

"I just..." Her face tightened, and she kept her eyes firmly on the road. "I don't want to talk about it, all right?"

"Can't you have children?" Once again, Rowena's reputation reared its ugly head. Maybe that's why she hadn't married yet. Titled men needed heirs.

"I..." She glanced pointedly in the rearview mirror.

Jake turned to check on Sammy, who was absorbed in an antique toy soldier Rowena had borrowed from the palace nursery. His son was paying them no attention whatsoever. Rowena was not going to find an out there. "He's not listening."

"How do you—"

"Rowena, is that it? Can you not have children?"

The look she finally threw at him would've melted Jake on the spot if he were ice cream. "Why are you interrogating me? Am I on the witness stand? Have I done something wrong?"

"No, of course not." Jake settled back against his seat again, but didn't take his eyes off her. He had no idea why knowing this was so important to him. But somehow, it was. "I'd just like to know."

"At the risk of being rude, *Mr. Stanbury,* the state of my reproductive organs is none of your business."

He stared at the delicate curve of her cheek. "Why do you always do that?"

"What?"

"Anytime I ask something personal, you call me Mr. Stanbury."

"That's your name, isn't it?"

Jake was too good a lawyer to be sidetracked. "You're trying to remind me that you're my employee. It's as if you…"

He trailed off.

It's as if she hid behind her servant's mask. As if she held it up like a shield anytime someone tried to get close. The way she had done the other night when he'd suggested she read in the library.

He frowned. That didn't jive with the image he had of her. Someone wanting to marry a title would play down—not emphasize—her lower status.

"As if I what?"

But now that he thought about the times he'd seen Rowena in a roomful of people, she'd been flitting around, yes, but there seemed to be a method to her flightiness. She would talk to every man in the room—except him, of course—but only for a moment. And she was usually carrying a tray of something, using it as a barrier between her and the men obviously interested in her.

It was as if she knew that behind her shield, she could flirt all she wanted…and still be safe.

"As if what?" she repeated.

He met her worried glance until her gaze was pulled back by the demanding road.

He didn't want to play this hand just yet. He needed to test his theory…to see if he could determine her motivation. As a lawyer, he'd learned that motivation was everything. With the right motivation—right, at least, in their minds—

people were capable of committing terrible crimes...even against themselves.

He knew Rowena wouldn't be satisfied with a brush-off, so he'd distract her by making her angry. "As if you enjoy being a servant. As if you love pointing out your inferiority."

On cue, she bristled. "I'm not inferior. Just different."

"What does that mean?"

"It means I'm a nanny, and you're a prince."

"I'm American. Americans don't have titles."

"You're fourth in line for the throne. Third if the king..."

She couldn't finish the sentence, and he couldn't blame her, but for another reason. "The last thing in the world I want is the throne of Edenbourg."

She glanced at him carefully. "You don't want to be king?"

"No."

"Why not?"

"I just quit one high-stress job so I could raise my son. I certainly don't want to jump in the middle of one with twenty-four-hour stress."

She brought the car to a halt at the entrance to a roundabout and studied him as if she couldn't decide whether or not she could believe him. Her expression reminded him of his suspicion about why she'd been placed in his household. Was she there to ascertain his involvement in the king's disappearance...or just to take care of his son?

"It's a lot of money," she pointed out as she eased into the empty roundabout.

He shrugged. "I have plenty of money."

"Not this much. Just think about how much the crown jewels are worth."

"You mean the fabulous riches locked up in some vault somewhere that no one can enter but the king and his heir, enough to buy the world two times over?"

"Yes."

He snorted. "I don't believe it exists. Edenbourg's economic status isn't now and has never been *that* good."

"How do you know?"

Jake considered what to tell her. He'd helped his father with the details of the trade agreement between Edenbourg and the United States, though Edward had taken all the credit for the success of the international pact. Since his father wanted to keep it that way, Jake said as little as he could get away with. "I did some research several months ago."

"On what? Edenbourg?"

"Yes, of course."

"Why?"

"Call it genealogical curiosity."

"Isn't economic strength an odd thing to research? Why not the history, or the landscape, or the tourism?"

"I researched those, too. But I was in mergers and acquisitions. Economics is what I'm interested in, what I know."

"Ena?"

Rowena blinked, then put on her happy face to glance at the back seat. "What Sammy?"

"Ena, how far to puppies?"

As Rowena replied, Jake listened to the exchange between them with half an ear. She'd come within a hairbreadth of asking him if he was involved in his uncle's disappearance.

He sat back, frustration keeping him stiff. She'd asked outright the other day at breakfast, and he'd answered her. Truthfully.

Obviously she didn't believe him. She still thought he was so greedy for Edenbourg's throne that he would do God knows what to a man who'd never harmed him, a man who was a blood relative.

Jake knew he shouldn't care what Rowena thought. He

would be leaving Edenbourg. Soon, he hoped. Chances are he'd never see her again.

But he did care.

He didn't want her to see herself as his employee...and he certainly didn't want her to think ill of him.

Which meant he was beginning to care about more than her skills as a nanny.

Damn.

Seton Wilde leaned against the door of the small, picturesque barn nestled against the side of a small mountain. "Puppies and children. There's not a happier sound in the world."

Rowena turned from her father to where she'd just left Sammy and Jake playing with the puppies in the straw of the unoccupied stall next to her father's Hackney, an award-winning harness racer.

Sammy lay back in the straw, giggling hysterically as he was attacked by six lively puppies intent on licking every part of him they could reach.

Jake sat next to Sammy, placing the puppies back on him if they wandered away. From the grin on his dark, handsome face, he was having as good a time as his son.

"Who couldn't love puppies?" she asked.

"Who couldn't love children?" her father countered.

Rowena sighed. "Yes. Those, too."

"So?"

Rowena feigned innocence, as if she didn't know what was coming. "So?"

"So...when are you going to make me a grandpa?"

She glanced pointedly at the afternoon sky broken only by puffs of white clouds. "I don't see any pigs flying, do you?"

"Pigs fly all the time." He grinned. "When you least expect it there they are, darkening the sky like bats."

She frowned at him. "I assume you want me to be married first?"

"That's usually how it's done."

"Not all the time."

"In our family, it is."

"That's the trouble. In order to have children, I have to be married. In order to be married, there has to be a man involved."

He chuckled. "Well, I've heard of different arrangements, but I don't think you lean that way."

She did lean, but only against the other door of the barn. "Sometimes I wish I did. It might be easier."

"Not if you want to have a baby."

She sighed heavily. "No."

Her father pushed away from the barn door. He walked over and positioned himself behind her so he could rub her shoulders the way he did when she was a little girl. "I know that man gave you a hard time a few years back, but not all men are like that."

Rowena didn't reply. They'd had this argument before. She just leaned into her father's massaging hands. His fingers could always work magic on her tight muscles.

"Take this Stanbury fellow, for instance."

"You take him," she muttered.

"Oh, I think he's more your type."

"Papa..."

"I've seen the way you look at him. And I've seen the way he looks at you. There's interest on both sides. You can't tell me there's not." He chuckled. "Tensing up. That's a good sign."

"A good sign?" She glared over her shoulder. "Of what?"

"That he's getting to you." He shook her shoulders. "Relax."

She obeyed, letting her head fall forward as his fingers

worked up her neck. "He's not getting to me, Papa. He's three places away from the throne, and you know how fond I am of royals."

"You like Isabel."

Rowena dismissed the comment with the wave of her hand. "Isabel is a woman. I'm talking about the men. Besides, Jake's under suspicion for the king's disappearance."

"Pshaw. That man wouldn't hurt a hair on anyone's head. Look at him with his boy. And see how gentle he is with the puppies?"

"Yes, well, I'm sure there are serial murderers who've had soft spots for animals."

"Actually, I read someplace that serial killers tend to torture small animals."

Rowena moaned softly. She didn't need her father pointing out Jake's gentle nature. She'd seen too much of it herself.

Her father paused in his ministrations. "Do you really believe this man murdered the king?"

Rowena peered up through her hair. Jake had a puppy in each hand and one yawning in his lap. They looked so tiny in his large hands, yet they were obviously not afraid of him, since one of them was gnawing on his thumb.

Sammy crawled through the straw beside Jake, three puppies following him yipping their cute little puppy yips.

Was this man capable of murder?

"No." The word came out before it consciously registered in her brain.

Her father patted her back, then continued rubbing it. "I knew you had the sense to recognize a good man when you see him."

She frowned. Her father was president of the local bank, and over the years had proven a nearly infallible judge of people. She'd always valued his opinion—especially since he'd been the only one to warn her about Heinrich.

"Is Jake Stanbury a good man?" she asked quietly.

Her father went still, as if taking a moment to study the man in question. Finally, he said, "I'd bet my last coin on it."

"Would you bet the bank's last coin?"

"In a heartbeat."

Rowena moaned. Great. Just great. Now what was she going to do?

Jake had been hard enough to resist when she thought he might be a criminal. Now that she was ninety-nine-point-nine percent certain he wasn't, it was going to be next to impossible.

Chapter Four

It was in the last place she looked.

Shock and dread immobilizing her, Rowena stared down at the copy of the ancient document lying on the rich grain of the graceful walnut desk sent to Edenbourg by Queen Anne herself.

During the week she'd been living in the cottage, she'd searched the house a little each day during Sammy's nap. When her search had come up empty, day after day, the only thing she had found was a deeper belief in Jake's innocence...which brought her deeper under his spell.

Now she'd found this.

The paper resting beneath her fingers was more than a microfiche copy of faded parchment. It was a neon sign pointing in bright flashing letters to Jake's culpability. Not proof, exactly, but an indication that he had a strong interest in the throne of Edenbourg.

It was the Edenbourg Treatise, written in 1468 by King Braden, which included among other things, the terms of ascendancy to the Edenbourg throne.

She'd just checked with the Edenbourg Archives. Jake had asked for a copy of it himself, in his own name, only four months ago.

Rowena started when the phone in her hand blared suddenly, complaining because she hadn't broken the connection from the call. She dropped the receiver back in its cradle, then tapped the hard black plastic with her strong, unpainted nails.

She should call Isabel immediately.

She glanced at the clock on the mantle. Two-fifteen.

She also needed to straighten the files she'd been rifling through. Sammy would probably be waking from his nap soon.

Instead, she leaned back in the tufted damask-upholstered desk chair and closed her eyes.

Why would Jake want a copy of the rules of succession unless he was planning to take over the throne...by whatever means necessary?

She couldn't come up with an answer. At least, not one that she liked.

He'd requested the information a few months before King Michael disappeared. That—added to the fact that he'd shown up in Edenbourg the day the king disappeared and was the first at the scene of the accident—was one coincidence too many.

So why could she still not grasp the fact that he was guilty?

"Stop it, Rowena." Her spine stiffened with resolve. "You know exactly why you don't believe he's guilty, and you've got to get over it."

With brisk motions, she set about straightening the files she'd easily found when she'd slipped into the library an hour ago.

She'd been warned about Heinrich, too. Papa had told her the prince from Leuvendan was no good after the first time the two met. She obviously had no sense where men were concerned, at least the ones she was attracted to.

This time, however, she was going to listen.

All she had to do was remember one fact: there was no happily ever after.

She knew this. She'd learned it the hard way, five years ago.

She had to trust her brain, and not her heart. Her heart let her down every time.

The Treatise went right back in with all the other papers. No need to keep this particular evidence. Anyone could have the proof of Jake's request with the same phone call she'd made.

When she finished, Rowena put everything on the desk back the way she'd found it, then rose to leave.

She paused at the door, looking back at the desk where Jake worked while he was home. Though she'd yet to see him sitting there, she knew his dark masculinity would overpower the graceful, feminine lines of the Queen Anne decor.

Hearing her own thought, she frowned as she closed the door.

How was she going to convince anyone else Jake was guilty, when she couldn't make herself believe it?

Jake slipped into the house a little after ten o'clock, weary from the endless discussions that always accompanied major trade negotiations—especially when there were bureaucrats involved.

He'd taken off his jacket and loosened his tie on the walk home, but it hadn't made him feel comfortable. As he lay his briefcase on the chest, he wondered how he could ever feel comfortable around people who considered him a suspect in his uncle's kidnapping.

Besides his father and Luke, his cousin Nicholas was the

only one who didn't watch him as if he had horns that would peek through his hair if a stray breeze blew in the window.

Jake rubbed his temples. He didn't drink much, but the benefits of a smooth glass of whiskey and a hot shower were too tempting to resist.

He stepped into the parlor and poured himself a neat shot of Scotland's finest. As the first sip burned a slow path down his throat, he settled into the nearest chair and pulled his tie completely off.

It didn't help matters that his father insisted on Jake making him look good. Not that Jake minded helping his father. It just made more work for everyone when he had to hold his thoughts on whatever point was being discussed until he could explain to his father what had been said and brief him on what to say so he could look as if he had a clue as to what was going on.

Two months ago, Edward had taken the credit for the trade deal between Edenbourg and the United States which Jake had salvaged from the mess his father had made of the negotiations.

It wasn't the first time Jake had pulled his father out of a tight scrape. Seemed like the only time Jake heard from his father was when Edward needed his son's legal expertise.

Jake took another sip of whiskey and forced his thoughts away from the negotiations.

The first thing he noticed was the quiet. He could hear waves lapping against the rocks at the bottom of the cliff, though the windows were shut tight.

Then he noticed the darkness. The only lights on that he could see were in the front foyer and a lamp here in the parlor.

Sammy would be asleep at this hour, but what about Rowena? Was she upstairs again, reading in bed?

Just the suggestion of Rowena in bed brought a vision of

her lying amid rumpled sheets in the bedroom next to Sammy's—just down the hall from his.

Jake took another sip of whiskey, then closed his eyes to savor the mental picture.

She would sleep naked, of course, and the sheet would barely cover the essentials…tantalizing him with slender curves…making him want to reach out and slowly pull the sheet—

Damn.

He shifted in the chair. At least one part of him wasn't tired.

Jake drained the whiskey and stood. He placed the glass on the cabinet serving as a bar, then made his way upstairs.

A lamp was burning in the room he'd occupied for just over a month, but first he slipped into Sammy's. He'd given his son a kiss every night since he was born, if he was home. If he was out of town, Jake called to tell him goodnight on the phone.

Even if Sammy was asleep, oblivious to his father's display of affection, Jake kept up the habit. If nothing else, it soothed him. And he felt that on some level, his son was aware that his father was there, in the night, loving him.

The door opened silently into the dark room. The light from his own room spilled in enough to guide Jake to his son's bed.

Sammy had been tucked in tightly and was curled on his side, facing the window.

Knowing a parade could march through the room and Sammy wouldn't stir, Jake sat on the side of the bed, then leaned over and placed a gentle kiss on his son's cheek.

"I love you, Sammy," he whispered.

"He knows."

The soft words startled Jake, and he turned toward the sound. His eyes had adjusted enough to see a dark figure outlined in the window on the other side of the bed.

"Rowena." The quiet word sounded intimate there in the dark. "Why are you sitting in here with the lights off?"

There was a noticeable hesitation before she said, "I haven't been here long. Sammy woke up about an hour after he fell asleep, so I read him another story."

Unaccountably pleased that she wasn't hidden in her room, Jake leaned over and turned on the lamp on his side of Sammy's bed. He wanted to see her.

She sat in the rocking chair, still dressed in the long, flowing blue-flowered dress he'd seen her in earlier. He'd yet to see her in a pair of pants, which added to the aura of femininity that drew him as nectar draws hummingbirds.

"I thought you'd gone to bed," he said.

"No."

"I guess it's not that late."

"Not compared to palace hours."

"Yes, but does the palace wake up as early as a two-year-old boy?"

"Not the royal family. Or at least, not very often. But the staff is stirring long before Sammy wakes up."

"You among them?"

"Not very often." She shrugged. "But sometimes. Depends on what time I went to bed the night before, and what Isabel needs me to do that day."

Her mention of going to bed in the palace did not bring the same stirring vision he'd had earlier. It made him wonder how many men she'd had in that bed.

If he believed the palace buzz, there were vast numbers.

On the other hand, if she was such a wanton, searching desperately for a husband with a title, why didn't she come on to him? Not that he had a title, but he was fourth in line for the throne to her country. From the things she'd said, that seemed to mean a lot to her. And it wasn't as if she didn't know he was attracted to her.

Knowing this wasn't the time or place for such an intimate

discussion, Jake turned the subject to a safer topic. "Was Sammy any trouble today?"

Her lips lifted in a weary smile. "Children are always trouble. But no. Not anything worth mentioning. He's such a sweet boy. I can see why you're proud of him."

Her praise meant more to him than all the contract points he'd ever won. "Thank you."

She placed a hand on the book in her lap and tensed, as if about to rise.

Wanting to keep her with him just a moment longer, Jake quickly asked, "What story did you read to him?"

She leaned forward and handed the book across the bed.

He touched the worn edges. "*The Princess and the Dragon.* This isn't one of his, is it?"

"No, I brought it with me. My mother used to read it to me when I was little. I thought Sammy would enjoy it. There's a battle between the dragon and the evil king."

Jake thumbed through the colorful pages. "Sounds violent."

"No more than other fairy tales."

He reached the end and read, "And they lived happily ever after."

"Don't they always?"

Her voice held such derision, he turned to her. "You don't believe people can live happily ever after?"

She gave him a pitying smile. "The sentiment is fine for children's fairy tales. But we both know happily ever after doesn't exist in the real world."

He never would've believed Rowena could be so cynical. What had happened to make her that way? "We do?"

She frowned. "Don't tell me that you—of all people— believe in happily ever after."

"Why me of all people?"

"You're divorced, aren't you?"

"Yes."

"Your father has been divorced three times, hasn't he?"

"Done a lot of research on us, have you?"

She ignored his comment. "How does any of that make you believe in happily ever after?"

Jake glanced down at his son. "He makes me believe it."

"Sammy?"

He nodded, then looked back at her. "I may not have experienced it myself, but I believe it's out there. I have to believe it. For Sammy."

"Believing doesn't make it happen."

"Maybe not, but hard work can. And if you don't believe, you'll never have it."

She regarded him as if he'd suddenly turned purple and sprouted antennae. "What do you mean, 'hard work?' Happily ever after either is or it isn't. Love either is or it isn't. And most of the time it isn't. People mistake sexual attraction for love."

He shook his head. "That's because they don't want to work at it. Love is hard work. I know. I've been working harder since I quit the law firm to be with Sammy than I ever did negotiating international trade deals."

She dismissed his comment with a graceful flick of her hand. "Children are easy to love. Especially your own child."

He gave her a crooked smile. "You haven't seen him at his worst. When he's tired and cranky and nothing makes him happy. Just wait. If you're around long enough, you'll see how hard it is."

"So what happened with your marriage? You didn't work hard enough?"

She had a mind like a lawyer. "It takes *two* people working hard at the right things to make a marriage last."

"Your wife, of course, is the one who wasn't working."

He lifted a shoulder. "Like I said, it takes two."

"Meaning...?"

"Meaning I'm sure I made my contributions."

Rowena leaned back in the rocking chair. "So now you're searching for happily ever after."

"No. I'm *creating* happily ever after...for Sammy." Jake rubbed his son's back. "He deserves it. And it's my responsibility as his father to see that he has it. I want him to have it."

Her frowned deepened. "So you're trying to find—"

Sammy murmured in his sleep, and turned over.

"We're disturbing him." Relief was clear in her voice as she rose. "And as you pointed out, I need to get some sleep if I'm going to keep up with him tomorrow."

Jake stood and watched Rowena tuck Sammy's covers in tighter, then place a gentle kiss on his cheek. He couldn't help but note the stark difference in her manner with him and then with Sammy.

What had caused—

She glanced up from the bed, and he saw what could only be bitterness in her eyes. And he knew.

Men had the power to hurt her. Boys did not.

But he hadn't hurt her...had he?

Still, cynicism such as she'd displayed came only from those who've been bitterly disappointed. Those who believed in something strongly only to have their beliefs shredded to pieces.

She straightened and smiled tightly. "Goodnight, Mr. Stanbury."

His brow lifted. So they were back to formality. "Goodnight, *Miss Wilde.*"

She hesitated, as if she wanted to argue further, then gave him a curt nod and slipped from the room.

Jake turned to switch off the light, but his attention caught on the book still on the bed. He lifted it and gazed down at the picture. Except for bright red hair, the princess looked amazingly like Rowena...complete with hazel eyes.

"What dragon shredded your heart?" he asked the picture.

There was no reply.

Chapter Five

Working at his desk early the next morning, Jake picked up the phone on the first ring. "Hello?"

"Hello, Jake. I'm glad I caught you."

His attention snapped away from the papers on the desk. "Annette."

"I wasn't sure of the time difference...or what you do over there to keep yourself amused...or out of jail."

Her voice held the same purring quality it always did when she was pleased about something. During their marriage, those somethings had rarely been good news for him.

"Very funny. What do you want? More money? Sorry. Your coils have squeezed every dime out of me you're going to get."

"I would think—living in the lap of luxury as you are— you could spare your poor ex-wife a few thousand."

"What's the matter? Good old Mikie's not rich enough?" Jake knew better. Michael Warrell was parked in the top fifty on the *Forbes* list of the richest men in America. "Or did you bleed him as dry as you bled me? How many lovers have you gone through since we divorced? Three? Four?"

"For your information, I'm no longer seeing Michael," she huffed. "As a matter of fact, I'm getting married."

There was a long pause. She was trying to make him ask, but he wasn't going to play her games anymore.

"No curiosity as to whom?" Not even the barest hint of exasperation showed in her voice.

He'd always admired her for having complete control over her emotions...assuming she had any to begin with.

"Not a damn bit," he replied.

"Bartholomew Stone the Fourth."

"And I would give a damn because...?"

"He's only the richest man in Virginia. He'll inherit his father's Senate seat when he retires next year."

"Senate seats are not inherited, Annette."

"This one will be." Her voice was smug.

Jake just wanted to get off the phone. "Congratulations. I have a lot of work to do, so—"

"But that's not why I called."

"Why am I not surprised?"

"I called about Sammy."

"Sammy?" Jake straightened in the tufted chair. In the year and a half since they'd divorced, they'd had numerous conversations...mostly arguments about how much money he was going to give her. But never—not one time—had she ever asked about her son. "What about him?"

"I'm concerned about my baby, living over there in that foreign country."

He leaned back stiffly. "*You,* concerned about Sammy? Don't tell me. The mules in Virginia have sprouted wings, right?"

"I'm serious, Jake."

She wanted something.

"How much is 'serious' going to cost me?"

"I want Sammy."

"No."

"I can take him, you know."

His eyes narrowed. "You signed full custody over to me."

"Yes, but in our agreement there's a clause about you not taking him out of the country without my permission."

"I told you I was bringing him over here."

"Can you prove you told me?"

"Can you prove I didn't?"

"You told me you were going on a vacation. You didn't tell me you were going to keep him out of the country indefinitely." There was a smirk in her voice as she added, "You didn't tell me your vacation plans included kidnapping the King of Edenbourg."

"Very funny. Just a regular clown today, I see."

"I'm not being funny. I'm very concerned about my son living with a father who could do such a thing."

Rage flowed through Jake like white-hot lava. "Why are you threatening me? You don't want Sammy. You never did."

"You're wrong, Jake," Annette purred. "I love my little boy."

"It's for this Stone, isn't it? Something about his election."

"Absolutely not. Though he did mention it would help if I showed voters the loving mother side of my personality."

"Your personality has many sides, Annette. Loving mother is not one of them."

"Cruelty will get you nowhere, Jake."

She had him, and she knew it. And to make things worse, he only had himself to blame. He'd written that damned custody agreement. The clause about taking the children out of the country was a standard one. He'd included it in case Annette decided to fight him at the last minute.

"How much do you want, Annette?"

"You're not going to buy your way out of this one, Jake. Sor-ree."

If they'd been having this conversation face-to-face, he would've had to overcome his baser instincts to keep from throttling the sing-song right out of her voice.

"I'm going to fight you."

"I know. But it won't matter. I'll be the married one. Even you know that judges look more favorably on the spouse with a stable, two-parent home. Especially when the judge is a fishing buddy of your father-in-law's."

"How much do you want?"

"I mean it, Jake sugar. This time you can't buy me off."

"Annette—"

"You'll be hearing from Bartholomew's lawyers within a few weeks. Ta ta."

The line went dead.

Jake slammed the receiver into the cradle, as if he could smash through Annette's threat.

The violence didn't help. He leaned his elbows on the desk and rubbed his temples.

She didn't want Sammy. He knew Annette well enough to know that she should never have been a mother.

He almost regretted bribing her into having a baby. But then he wouldn't have had Sammy. And Sammy was worth every piece of dirt Annette had ever thrown at him.

She couldn't do it. He wouldn't let Annette get her clutching claws on Sammy. He'd do anything—*anything*—to keep his son safe.

"So you found something?"

Princess Isabel took Rowena's arm and dragged her toward the French doors leading onto the terrace.

Rowena glanced over her shoulder to make sure Sammy was okay. He sat on the nursery floor with his great-aunt,

Queen Josephine. She was showing him a photo album of all the babies who'd stayed in the royal nursery.

Sammy seemed entranced by the children's faces, especially since his own was going to be added to the book.

Rowena stepped through the French doors to join Isabel. The princess leaned back against the waist-high balustrade overlooking the palace gardens, but was by no means at ease.

"Did you bring it with you?" she asked. Her voice was low-pitched enough so no one in the nursery or the garden below could hear her.

Rowena answered the same way. "No. You can get the same evidence with a phone call."

"Is it hard evidence?" Isabel asked. "Is he guilty?"

Rowena shook her head. "It's no more conclusive than what we have already."

"So what did you find?"

"Four months ago, he requested a copy of the Edenbourg Treatise from the archives."

Isabel straightened. "That lays out the rules of ascendancy."

"Yes."

"Why would he want that...unless he wanted to be certain that his father would inherit the throne if my father and Nicholas were out of the way."

To hide her frown, Rowena stepped over to lean against the balustrade, but facing the garden. Isabel had come to the same conclusion she had. "Yes. Why indeed?"

Isabel turned to face the same way as Rowena. "But you're right. It's as circumstantial as everything else we have on him. Not even worth presenting to the police. There wasn't anything else?"

"No."

"You didn't ask him about it, did you?"

"Of course not. Then he'd know I was looking." She sighed and splayed her fingers across the warm stone. "I'm not so sure that he doesn't already know. Or at least suspect.''

Isabel shook her head. ''He would've said something, I think. Jake does not seem like the kind of man to keep quiet about having his privacy violated.''

Rowena's frown deepened. What would Jake say if he caught her? She shivered, despite the warmth of the late April sun. That's one thing she did not want to find out.

''He did tell me—when we were talking about something else—that he'd been doing research on Edenbourg.''

''Did he say why?''

She shrugged. ''He called it 'genealogical curiosity.'''

''Hmmm.'' Isabel leaned her long, graceful arms on the balustrade. ''I'm pretty curious myself. Curious to see how much 'genealogical' information he has.''

''If he has any more, it isn't at the cottage. I've gone over his bedroom and the library with a fine-tooth comb.''

''Perhaps in his apartment in New York.''

Rowena gave Isabel a hard look. ''You want me to go to New York?''

''No, of course not. You need to stay here and keep up the nanny pretense. In case something happens.'' Her lips curved in a pleased grin. ''I'll fly to the States and see what I can find. Did you find a key to his apartment while you were searching?''

Rowena straightened from the balustrade. ''Yes. Taped to a file, clearly labeled, as if he expects something to happen to him. But surely there's no need for you to go over there. Maybe I didn't look as hard as I thought. I'll go back through his papers as soon as I can and see if I missed anything.''

Isabel nodded. ''Yes. Do that. But I'm going to New York.''

Rowena placed a hand on the princess's arm. ''Your father forbade you to do things like that, remember?''

Isabel had served a tour in the royal navy, and had especially enjoyed her stint with military intelligence. She relished this kind of spy mission and had wanted to continue working with intelligence, but her father told her that her obligation was to act like a royal princess, not to risk her neck.

Isabel lifted her chin. "Papa isn't here, is he? Which is exactly the point."

"If he knew I let you go—"

"If he knew, then that would mean he was home, which would mean my trip was successful. In which case, he'd reward you."

"Isabel..."

Isabel met her gaze squarely. Tears sparkled in the sunlight, turning her green eyes murky. "Please don't try to talk me out of it, Rowena. I *have* to do something."

Rowena knew how her friend felt. She missed the king, too. And she was in danger every day, if Jake was responsible for the king's disappearance. She was living with him...spying on him.

But she didn't feel like she was in danger. She felt...at home, living with Sammy and Jake. It felt comfortable... complete.

The revelation startled her. To avoid dealing with it, Rowena nodded to Isabel. "You're right. A month has gone by with no word from or about your father. It's time for drastic measures. I'll have a copy made of his key."

Isabel gave her a hug. "Thank you for understanding."

Rowena hugged her back. "Promise you'll call as soon as you're out of his apartment. I'll be worried sick until I hear from you."

"I'll call as soon as I walk out of his building. I—"

Suddenly, Rowena's knees were tackled. She grabbed the balustrade to keep from falling.

"Ena! Guess what?"

Rowena pasted on a smile and leaned down to pick up

her charge. As Sammy chattered on about gluing his picture in the book, she reviewed her conversation with Isabel.

She didn't think she'd mentioned Jake by name, but she wasn't sure. She was going to have to be a lot more careful.

She wasn't very good at this spy thing.

Later that afternoon, bored with the argument over the merits of a free-market economy, Jake stretched his neck and allowed his gaze to wander.

The April afternoon had been so alluring even to these hardened statesmen, they'd moved their meeting outdoors for tea.

Of course, nothing was simple for palace people. They didn't just drag folding chairs out under a tree. Within minutes of Nicholas expressing the wish to move outdoors, an awning had been erected. Beneath it, upholstered chairs sat on an oriental rug around a table complete with linen tablecloth, china and silver.

The same trusted footmen who hovered over them inside kept their cups full of tea and the trays of sandwiches, tarts and fruit overflowing.

What he wouldn't give for a hot dog and a beer.

Movement at the corner of his eye pulled his attention to a path leading to the palace. A small contingent of ladies ambled through the garden.

In the center strolled the queen, pushing an elaborate carriage no doubt containing her granddaughter, LeAnn. Queen Josephine was flanked by her pregnant daughter, Princess Dominique, and her daughter-in-law, Princess Rebecca. Princess Isabel brought up the rear, walking arm-in-arm with Rowena.

Jake's eyes narrowed. Where was—

A dark head popped above a low hedge.

Jake smiled in relief. Sammy was racing ahead of the women, jumping up to snatch at something. Was it too early for butterflies this far north? Sammy was fascinated by butterflies.

Jake wistfully watched the women meander in the warmth of the sun. He'd ten times rather be with them than here.

Satisfied Sammy was okay, Jake's eyes drifted back to Rowena. She seemed to be as much a member of the royal family as Isabel. The two of them walked several paces behind the queen, their heads close together.

Jake smiled. What were they discussing so intently? What Isabel thought about the latest pseudo-prince who'd shown up to murmur platitudes of concern over King Michael's disappearance?

Whatever it was, Isabel's face glowed.

Rowena's wore the bland mask he was coming to know meant she wasn't pleased by something.

Apparently Isabel liked her new beau, but Rowena disapproved.

Isabel should listen to Rowena. She was a good judge of character.

Jake frowned. Now why would he think that? She was the one who—according to palace rumor—dated countless men.

Although…he was beginning to seriously doubt the gossip. Not one ardent beau had shown up at his door in the middle of the night during the ten days she'd stayed at the cottage. And as far he knew, the only phone calls she received were from Isabel.

He wasn't usually so quick to believe such tales about anyone, preferring to draw his own conclusions from conversation and observation, if knowing that person was important.

Yet with Rowena, he'd latched onto the local gossip like a lifeline. And he knew why. He'd used it as a talisman against his attraction for her.

But it hadn't worked.

The queen paused in her stately walk to speak over her shoulder.

Rowena dropped a quick curtsey, said something to Isabel as she pointed ahead—probably about watching Sammy—then turned and headed back toward the palace at a quick pace.

Jake frowned. The little servant had been sent on an errand.

Though he knew that's what Rowena's job was, he didn't like it. She should be treated like…like a princess, not a servant.

He leaned his chair back, craning his neck to keep Rowena in sight through the trees. The filmy colors of her full skirt flowed behind her like butterfly wings.

Suddenly one foot was kicked out from under him, and his chair landed with a soft thud on all four legs.

Beside him, his father gave him a ''Behave or you'll get a spanking'' look.

Feeling like a kid chastened for not paying attention in mass, Jake bristled. He wanted to tell his father just where he could shove this pointless, political version of mass, but knew he couldn't. For Sammy's sake, he was trying to reconnect with his family…which meant Edward and Luke.

So he played the dutiful son and returned his attention to the proceedings. As he did, he intercepted a look from Prince Nicholas. His cousin smiled at him sympathetically, then shifted his gaze toward the women.

Jake smiled at the silent moment of communication. Nicholas was very much in love with his wife, Rebecca, and wasn't afraid to let it show.

In that moment, he knew that he and Nicholas had a lot in common. They both would rather be chasing butterflies.

''We're late, Sammy-Jammy.'' Rowena closed the front door behind him. ''And it's Mrs. Hanson's night off.''

Sammy skidded to a stop in the middle of the foyer. "No food?"

She smiled at the horror on his adorable face. "Are you hungry?"

He nodded vigorously.

"Well, you should be, as hard as you played this afternoon. We'll find something, don't worry. I'm glad your father's not home yet." She held a hand out to him as she moved toward the kitchen. "Did you have a good time this afternoon?"

He skipped along beside her, pulling on her arm. "Lan wasn't no fun. I like Neeki more."

Rowena laughed. "Well, Neeki—or as she's known in more formal circles, Princess Dominique—is a grown-up. LeAnn is just a baby. It will be at least a year before she's fun to—"

"About time you two got home."

"Eeek!" Rowena shoved Sammy behind her before she realized who was speaking. "Jake!" She held a hand over her fast-pumping heart. "You startled me."

She'd had too much spy talk with Isabel that afternoon.

Sammy peeked around her skirt. "Daddy, guess what?"

Jake held out his arms. "What?"

Sammy raced into his father's arms and giggled as he was thrown high in the air. When his father settled him on an arm, he said proudly, "I'm in a picture book."

"You are? What kind of picture book?"

"With dead people."

"Dead people?" Jake turned to Rowena for help.

"Did you just come out of the kitchen?" she asked.

"Yes, I did. Dead people?"

"Oh. There's a book in the royal nursery of all the children who've stayed there." Her hand slid from her heart to her hip. "What were you doing in the kitchen? Are you hungry? I'm sorry we're late, but Isabel—"

"I was fixing something for dinner." Jake bounced Sammy on his arm. "Sammy hasn't stayed in the royal nursery. He's been with me the whole time."

"But he probably will stay there at some point. Queen Josephine wants to have him spend the night sometime soon." Rowena stepped over and lifted his tie, which sported a mustard stain. "Did you say you're preparing dinner?"

"Yes. Do you think the stain will come out?"

"Probably not, but I'll try." She reached up to slip off the already loosened knot. "Take it off."

He turned away from her. "I'll do it."

She blinked. "What?"

He headed for the kitchen. "You heard me."

She followed. "Well, yes, but…"

"But what?"

Rowena had no idea what she'd been about to say, she was so shocked by what she saw. On the small table in the corner of the kitchen, dinner had been laid out…complete with tablecloth, napkins and silverware. A plate of sandwiches sat in the middle, with a bowl of potato salad and an array of pastries.

"Oh boy!" Sammy squirmed to be let down. "I'm hungry."

Jake set his son on the floor. "But what?"

Rowena lifted her gaze to his. "You made dinner?"

"No, the sea urchins scuttled up the cliff and set it out. I found it when I got home."

"But…but…"

"There you go with those buts again." He smiled and took away the pastry Sammy had grabbed. "This is for after you eat the sandwich."

"Oh, Daddy." Sammy climbed into the chair with his booster seat.

Jake stepped to the refrigerator and pulled out a glass of milk and a bottle of wine. "Is there a point to them?"

Rowena blinked. "To what?"

He grinned. "Your buts."

She cleared her throat. "You made dinner."

"Yes. I believe we already established that." He pulled out a chair and indicated that she should sit.

She complied automatically.

"It isn't much. I'm not the greatest cook, but I found a deli not too far from the palace." He sat in the chair next to hers. "Ready-made food always helps."

As he opened the wine, she stared at the table. "I can't believe you made dinner."

He chuckled. "Why does that amaze you?"

"Why did you?"

He met her gaze squarely. "You've been waiting on people all day. It's time someone waited on you."

He looked away to pour the wine before he could see the tears that sprang to Rowena's eyes. No one had ever waited on her, except when she ate out...and they were paid to do it.

"Ena, guess what?" Sammy already had a milk mustache.

She cleared the emotion from her throat. "What, Sammy-Jammy?"

"Dinner looks good."

"Yes, it does. It really, truly does."

Jake lifted his glass of wine to her. "To delis."

She lifted hers and clinked it against his. "To delis."

They each took a sip, then set down their glasses and reached for the food.

Dinner had never tasted so good.

Jake slipped into the house the next afternoon with a smile. Funny how the farther he got from the palace, the better he felt.

Especially when he'd been let out of mass early.

Especially when he had a wonderful son to come home

to…and a beautiful woman whose golden eyes lit up when he walked through the door.

The house was quiet as he set his briefcase on the chest in the foyer. Where was everyone?

He loosened his tie and unbuttoned his collar as he walked through the downstairs rooms. He glanced at the clock in the kitchen as he passed through. It was just after three. Maybe they'd gone to the palace. Although Rowena had specifically said they were going to have a quiet day at home.

And where was Mrs. Hanson?

She'd been here, because there was a plate of chocolate cookies on the counter, covered by wax paper.

He grabbed one and took a bite as he stepped through the laundry room and headed into the hall. He was not surprised the laundry was empty. Rowena was not responsible for any cleaning chores. Mrs. Hanson took care of those.

Jake paused with a hand on the library door and pushed the last bite of cookie into his mouth.

Though he didn't hear voices coming from the library, he turned the knob and pushed the door.

Then stopped dead in the doorway, his heart stopping with him.

Rowena's head shot up from the ravaged desk. She gasped. "Jake! What…what are you doing home?"

Chapter Six

Rowena froze, her hands full of Jake's papers...evidence incriminating her far more than anything she'd found to incriminate him.

"Where's Sammy?" he asked in a voice of ice.

"He's..." she swallowed the lump of shame in her throat "...napping."

"So he doesn't know you were sent to spy on me?"

"No, of course not."

"At least there's that." He closed the door behind him and walked slowly to the other side of the desk.

An instant of fear grabbed Rowena by the heart, but it quickly disappeared. She was not afraid of physical harm from Jake. That, more than anything, told her what she already knew...he wasn't guilty.

"Did you find what you were looking for?"

"I..." She carefully laid the papers that were still in her hand on the desk. "I wasn't looking for anything in particular."

"Just something to prove I kidnapped the king."

She winced at his bluntness. "Yes."

"But you didn't find anything."

She hesitated. The key to his apartment which she'd already slipped into a pocket burned a hole in her conscience. But there was something else. She slowly slipped the Edenbourg Treatise from its folder. "Just this."

As he took the copy from her hand, his cold blue gaze searched her face, then he looked down. He thumbed through the top couple of sheets, then glanced up with one eyebrow raised. "How, exactly, does this make me guilty?"

"It doesn't, really. It just—"

"How?"

She took a deep breath. "It lays out the rules of ascendancy to the throne of Edenbourg."

"Among other things." He dropped the Treatise on the desk. "So...in your mind, I'm making sure the throne will come to me—if I get rid of everyone ahead of me in line."

"Well...I suppose...something like that. But not in my—"

"Which includes my uncle, my cousin, my father and my brother."

Her shrug was more jerky than nonchalant.

"This wouldn't constitute evidence in any court in the United States."

"Here, either," she quickly added. "But you have to admit, it looks bad. You ordered a copy—in your own name—just a few months before you came to Edenbourg for the first time."

"In my own name. Exactly. If I were planning to kidnap the king, would I have used my own name? Don't you think I'm just a little smarter than that?" He splayed his fingertips on the desk and leaned on them heavily. "I ordered this copy through the inter-library loan department, for God's sake. Anyone with a library card can get one."

"I know." Her voice sounded very small. "I didn't say it was much. I said it was all I found."

With a muttered curse, he turned away and strode over to stare out the curtainless window overlooking the North Sea.

Rowena stood where she'd been caught, unable to take a step in any direction. She wasn't afraid of Jake, but she was afraid to move. She knew that when she did, she'd be moving out of the house.

She'd betrayed his trust. They'd become…very good friends in the two weeks she'd been living in the cottage. They'd laughed together, and shared Sammy stories…and looks that probably sent steam billowing up the chimneys.

Jake felt like family. He felt like…home.

Rowena sucked in a tiny breath. Dear God. Was she falling in love with him?

No. She couldn't. Though he didn't carry the title of prince, he was one.

Fear got her moving.

She stepped around the desk and headed for the door. "I'll pack my things."

"No."

His voice stopped her six feet from the door…from safety. When he didn't say anything more, she turned to face him.

He hadn't moved from the window. "Sammy loves you. It would break his heart if you left so abruptly. And I wouldn't know what to tell him."

She spread her hands, even though he was still staring out the window. "You could tell him Isabel needs me."

Finally he turned to face her. "That's supposed to satisfy a two-year-old?"

"He's nearly three." Even Rowena knew her argument was lame.

He stared at her for an endless time. His blue eyes had turned from ice to the hottest part of fire…and she wasn't certain it was all anger.

To hide the shiver that passed along her spine, she took a step toward him. "Jake…"

"Don't."

She wrapped her arms around herself. Why did she have to search his office today? Why did she have to search it again at all? She'd found all there was to find the first time.

If she could turn back the clock, she'd lie down with Sammy and nap with him. Anything to keep from seeing the accusation in Jake's eyes.

Finally, she couldn't stand the ponderous silence any longer. "Is this how you make the people on the witness stand crack? Staring at them until they confess everything?"

He did not appear to be amused.

"Say something. Please."

"I was not a trial lawyer."

"Oh. That's right. Mergers and acquisitions."

"You were sent here to spy on me." The attack was sudden, and went right for her jugular.

She flinched and put her hand to her throat. "Well, yes, partly."

"Partly?"

"I've done a whole lot more nannying than spying."

"That's supposed to make me feel better?"

Her hands dropped back to her waist. "No. I'm sorry. Yes. That was the plan. I was supposed to see if there was anything here that might link you—or your father or brother—to the king's disappearance."

"Isabel put you up to it. I thought she was supposed to be your friend."

"Isabel is the best friend I have in the—"

"What if I *had* been the one who kidnapped the king, and I caught you? Where would you be then?"

She swallowed hard. "Probably on the rocks at the base of the cliff by now."

With four steps, he invaded her space. "Don't get cute

with me. How could you risk your life doing something you have no idea how to do?''

Rowena couldn't take her gaze from his angry face. But he wasn't angry at her. Not really. He was angry *for* her. Which meant he cared.

She felt a strange fluttering in her chest, as if a thoroughly tightened knot had suddenly been untied.

Which wasn't good. It meant she cared that he cared.

She needed to find that knot and retie it as soon as possible.

''I did it for Isabel. She's trying to exonerate her brother.''

Jake's eyes narrowed even more. ''Always the dutiful little servant, aren't you?''

''What's wrong with that?''

''Damn it, Ena! If she asked you to jump off the cliff, would you? How far were you prepared to take this? Would you have slept with me, hoping I'd talk in my sleep?''

He called her Ena. No one else but Sammy called her that. While not a declaration of love, the diminutive was clearly affectionate.

''Not for Isabel.'' She held her breath. Had she really been so bold?

Jake's eyes were blue lasers, burning all the way through to her bones. She felt the heat, reveled in it, let it swirl into every corner of her being. It drove out every shred of resistance, every awareness of the royal blood flowing through his veins. All she saw was a man. A man who wanted her. A man she wanted just as much.

As if the thought could make it happen, suddenly she was in his arms. His lips descended on hers, and she stood on tiptoe to meet him halfway.

No sweet first kiss, with tentative meeting of the lips. This was powerful, unrestrained. Their mutual, acute desire sent shock waves pounding through her, agitating every cell in her body, making her blood roil through her veins.

She wrapped her arms around his neck to pull him closer.

He moaned, and tightened his arms, lifting her until her toes dangled just above the floor.

She felt as if she were flying.

When they finally had to part to feed lungs demanding air, he set her on the floor and rested his forehead against hers.

"Damn." He panted hard for a moment, then said, "I have a question."

She opened her eyes to see him peering at her intently. "Yes?"

"Do you really believe I kidnapped the king?"

She shook her head. "No."

He drew back several inches. "Then why were you searching my desk?"

"To satisfy Isabel. I knew I wouldn't find anything."

"Are you saying that because you're still dazed by my kisses, because you're afraid of me, or because you mean it?"

"Would I kiss you if I thought you were guilty?"

"I don't know how far you'd go...for Isabel."

She sighed. "I suppose I deserve that."

He frowned. "I'm sorry. I shouldn't..."

She placed a finger on his lips. "I have never, ever been with a man for Isabel. I never would, and she would never ask."

"Why?"

She blinked. "Why wouldn't she ask?"

He shook his head. "Why do you believe I'm not the man who kidnapped the king?"

Her gaze dropped to his throat as she considered his question. "When I first moved in, I thought it was because I'm...attracted to you."

There. She'd admitted it...out loud.

He lifted her chin and searched her eyes. "How long?"

She didn't pretend she didn't know what he was asking. Still, she'd been denying her desire so long, it was hard to discuss. But she knew him well enough by now to know he wouldn't be satisfied with less than everything. "Since the first time I saw you."

Satisfaction gleamed in his eyes. "Interesting. All right. We'll discuss that in a minute."

With her chin high in the air, it was difficult to swallow. "Do we have to?"

"Oh, yes. We definitely have to." His legally trained mind went back to the original line of questioning. "So what you're saying is that you've never believed I kidnapped my uncle."

"That's right."

He smiled and released her chin. "And living with me for a couple of weeks hasn't changed your mind."

She nodded. "You would never have done anything to harm your uncle."

"How can you be so sure?"

"I've seen how much family means to you. Especially Sammy. I haven't really seen you with your father and brother, but you're with them nearly every day. You don't even seem to resent the queen and Prince Nicholas and Princesses Dominique and Isabel—even though they've kept you in Edenbourg against your will. Even though they believe you could be guilty."

He shrugged. "I know they're only doing what they have to. As far as thinking I'm guilty, they don't know me. Not like you know me."

She frowned. "I don't know you either, Jake."

"Oh, yes, you do. You've lived with me, seen me every day. This is who I am." He pulled her closer. "You know me well enough to be attracted to me."

"Proximity and time don't mean very much, I'm afraid. I was attracted to you before I even knew your name."

He chuckled. "Now that you do, do you want me any less?"

She sucked in a breath. "Want you. You mean sexually, don't you?"

"That's what attraction is…when you don't even know someone's name. Now, I hope, it goes beyond that."

She drew away, but he wouldn't let her go. "No, Jake. I can't. *We* can't."

"Why not? We're both free, we're both willing, and we're both adults. Where's the harm?"

Since she couldn't get free, Rowena hid her face against his chest. She pulled the rich, warm smell of him in with every breath. The deeply sensuous aroma swirled around her brain, zapping her ability to think.

For a moment, she considered giving in to the numbing heat, to sink into Jake and give him everything she wanted to give him, everything he wanted to take.

But she couldn't. The pain of her experience with Heinrich had cut too deep. Jake was a member of the royal Stanburys. She was a mere lady-in-waiting. He would make love to her, then leave her as soon as the authorities pronounced him innocent.

Where's the harm?

The harm would be to her heart.

"Don't hide from me." He pulled back far enough to lift her chin. "What's wrong?"

"I'm your employee. Even in the States, that's frowned upon."

A thundercloud passed over his face. "Why do you keep harping on that? You're *not* my servant."

"I'm nanny to your son. What else would you call it?"

"Do I sign your paycheck?"

"Well…technically, I guess Isabel still does, but…"

"Then you're not my employee."

"If I'm not, what am I?"

His face softened. "You're a beautiful woman who I admire tremendously, who I like more than any woman I've ever known and who I desire desperately."

The shiver that passed over her was equal parts pleasure and regret. "Jake, please. The gossips in the palace are already talking about me, about what I'm doing here."

"Who?" he demanded. "I'll set them straight."

"If we slept together, what would you tell them then?"

"That's it none of their damn business."

"You're right, it isn't. But they still talk."

"If they're talking anyway, what does it matter?"

"It matters to me."

He searched her eyes. "How can I keep on living here with you, knowing you want me as much as I want you. You do, don't you?"

Though she tried, he wouldn't let her look away. "I've never wanted a man...like this."

Their lips came together as if pulled by sorcery. Rowena gave herself to the magic, knowing she was lost, knowing she'd been lost since the moment she saw him.

If he pushed the issue, she knew she'd follow him upstairs to his room.

Fortunately, he proved to be the man she thought he was.

He let go of her suddenly, cursing under his breath.

Stepping back, he demanded, "So what are the rules? Are we supposed to go on like before?"

He released her so suddenly, Rowena staggered, then caught herself with a hand on the back of a chair. When she recovered her equilibrium, his words penetrated. "Couldn't we be...friends?"

"Tell me, Ena. After kissing me like you did, could you be just my friend? Could you watch me walk in the door every evening and not want to kiss me again? Could you lie in your bed at night and not think of me in mine, just down the hall? Because I sure as hell don't think I can stop my thoughts about you.''

She winced, knowing he was right. ''Perhaps I should move back to—''

''No.'' His refusal was once again blunt, harsh, final.

''But if we can't—''

''It would be too disruptive for Sammy.''

His explanation made relief wash through her, which made her realize she was further gone than she thought. ''All right. So what do we do?''

He studied her face for a long moment, then eased himself onto the settee just behind him. ''I have a suggestion.''

''What?''

''I suggest that we collaborate.''

She peered at him hard. ''Isn't that just another word for—''

''I mean gathering information…about who kidnapped the king.''

It took a moment for Rowena's mind to grasp the change of subject. When it did, she stepped around the chair she'd been clutching and sank onto the hard cushion. Jake could obviously change gears in mid-thought, but it took her a minute. ''Collaborate?''

''Exactly. We both want to find who kidnapped the king. I want to clear my name. You want to clear Nicholas's. Let's work together.''

''Two heads are better than one…especially when one of them is a lawyer's.''

His mouth twisted. ''Going to start with lawyer jokes now, are you?''

''Well, I was being serious, but…'' She leaned back with a tiny smile. ''Why won't a shark ever bite a lawyer?''

He rolled his eyes. ''Professional courtesy. Believe me, I've heard them all. I see lawyers are treated with the same disrespect in Edenbourg as they are in the United States.''

"I think it's a universal revulsion. One of those cross-cultural emotions that pull all of humanity together." She grinned. "Sort of like hating the bogeyman, or the devil."

He leaned forward, eyes gleaming. "Want to see my... pitchfork?"

She did...desperately. But she knew any more teasing and they'd be in each other's arms again. While that would be far from unpleasant, it would be dangerous...and devastating. Though she no longer believed that Jake had kidnapped the king, he was more than capable of kidnapping her heart.

"Perhaps we'd better get back to the collaboration issue."

He raised a brow. "Do we have to?"

She quirked a brow back at him. Was he mocking her earlier cowardice, or her cowardice now? It didn't matter. It was much better to be safe than broken-hearted. It was how she'd survived the past five years. "I insist."

He leaned back. "Too bad."

"Do you really think it's a good idea?"

"Why not? You have connections at the palace, so you know what's going on in the investigation. We can discuss what they've found and perhaps a fresh mind will be able to see something they haven't."

"What about Isabel?" Rowena remembered the key in her pocket. The key Isabel would use to search Jake's apartment. Since she was agreeing to work with him, she should tell him about Isabel's plans, shouldn't she?

Rowena felt like a paper doll, torn down the middle. If she told Jake, he'd be angry all over again. And if he were guilty, he'd have time to have someone hide any evidence he'd left in his apartment. Though she felt, deep down, that he wasn't guilty, there was always the possibility she was wrong.

Better not to tell him. If Isabel finds something, he needs to be caught. But Rowena was certain the princess would come up as empty-handed as Rowena had.

In that case, Jake need never know.

"What about Isabel?" he asked.

She focused on his face. "Should I tell her we're working together?"

"You know her better than I do. I'll leave that up to you."

Rowena frowned at the picture on the wall behind Jake.

"Is that an 'I'll tell her' or an 'I won't tell her' face?"

Her gaze focused on his chiseled features. "I'd feel disloyal if I didn't tell Isabel. She's determined to clear her brother of suspicion. I'm afraid her heart's set on you being guilty. Mainly because you're all we've got. That's why she talked me into coming here."

Jake smiled wryly. "Sorry to disappoint her."

"On the other hand, Isabel is very fair. She's not going to accuse you without hard evidence. However, I'm afraid she's not going to believe you're *not* guilty without hard evidence, either."

"What you're saying is that if you tell her you think I'm not guilty without substantial proof, she'll think I seduced you."

"Yes." From the heat on her cheeks, Rowena knew she was blushing.

From the look in his eyes, Jake noticed. He seemed fascinated, as if he'd never seen anyone blush before.

Which, of course made her blush even more.

"And did I?" he asked softly.

"Yes." The word was little more than a sigh.

"Come here, Ena."

The diminutive sounded excruciatingly intimate on Jake's lips. She closed her eyes, as if that could shut out his powerful spell. As if. One second of Jake's raw, naked desire seduced her far more than all of Heinrich's flowery phrases. "No, Jake."

"Even if I have some…hard evidence to show you?"

She laughed, surprised by his frank words. She opened

her eyes to find him grinning at her lecherously. She had a feeling that making love with Jake would be more than sensuous...it would be fun.

And they lived happily ever after.

Rowena frowned. Why did those words pop into her head?

She didn't believe in happily ever after. It was just a line in fairy tales.

Then she remembered... Jake believed. He'd told her he was creating happily ever after for Sammy.

Rowena shivered.

The possibility of creating happily ever after with Jake was as seductive as his kisses.

She was going to have to be very careful...if she wanted to get out of this with her sanity—and her heart—intact.

Chapter Seven

Jake set his half-finished coffee on the patio table on the terrace of the Cottage and leaned back in the cushioned iron chair. He turned his face to the sun still an hour from setting, but the stiff breeze off the North Sea blew the rays away before they could heat his skin.

Did this tiny island ever get warm?

"Wonder why Luke couldn't make it tonight," his father commented from across the table.

Jake made a noncommittal sound. He didn't miss his brother.

"You're quiet tonight."

Jake finally opened his eyes to see his father wiping Mrs. Hanson's white chocolate Macadamia cake from his lips. He straightened reluctantly. "Sorry. I haven't been sleeping well the past few days. I guess everything's getting to me."

Edward cocked a brow toward the garden, where Rowena played with Sammy in a boisterous game of kickball. Their laughter had drifted over the railing all through dinner. "Anything to do with a certain nanny you've been throwing looks at?"

Jake was surprised by his father's astute observation. It wasn't like Edward Stanbury to notice anything about his younger son. "Of course not. I..."

Though they'd kept in touch over the years, Jake had never had a close relationship with his father. He'd never discussed anything as personal as his sex life or his marriage with Edward, and didn't know how to begin now.

"Yes?"

"I had a call from my ex-wife, is all."

"Ah." His father leaned back with his coffee. "Calls from ex-wives are never pleasant."

His father should know. He had three.

"No, they're not."

"Anything I can help you with? Or just the usual pestering for more money?"

"No, this time she doesn't want money." Jake glanced toward his son. "She wants Sammy."

"Well, let her have him for a while. You've been—"

"No." Jake's refusal was abrupt, hard. He should've known his father wouldn't understand. Edward had given him up, after all.

Edward set his coffee cup down. "I see."

Jake couldn't resist a jab. "Do you?"

Edward regarded him over steepled fingers. "If you think I don't, why don't you explain it to me?"

Jake was irritated with himself. He should've just let it go. "Annette doesn't want Sammy. She's marrying into a political family, and they want her to have a motherly image."

"You were awarded full custody, weren't you?"

"Yes, but there's a clause in the agreement that stipulates how long I can keep Sammy out of the country without her permission. I've exceeded that, and she's going to use it against me."

"Can she win?"

Jake shrugged, though he was far from indifferent. "Courts have traditionally favored spouses who are married over ones who are not, especially if that spouse is the mother. They seem to think it implies stability. Which shows they don't know Annette."

"So…get married yourself."

"Yeah, right."

"I'm not joking."

Jake stared at his father as Edward took another sip of coffee. "And just who would I marry?"

Though he couldn't see her, Rowena's face popped into his thoughts. Jake shook his head to clear it.

As if he could read Jake's mind, Edward looked meaningfully toward the garden. "What about the lovely nanny? You certainly can't say you'd mind having her in your bed for a while. I've seen you looking at her."

This conversation was insane. "I can't marry E… Rowena."

"Why not?"

"I'm not in love with her." As he said the words, they felt wrong. But he wasn't in love. He couldn't be…because he wasn't ever going to fall in love again. He'd promised himself. "We've only known each other a few weeks."

"So? I only knew Elizabeth a week before we married."

Elizabeth was his father's second wife. "And how long did that marriage last? Five years?"

"Six and a half. Most marriages don't last when the sex stops being good."

"They can."

Edward shrugged. "If you're lucky."

"Or work hard at it."

"Whatever. Sammy obviously adores this Rowena. And she's a pretty little thing. Why not?"

Why not, indeed?

Jake shook his head. "No. It's a shallow solution to a

serious problem. There has to be a legal solution. Don't worry, I'll find it.''

Half an hour later, Rowena carried a tired Sammy into the house. Their boisterous play had worn him out.

With her foot barely on the first step, she heard a knock on the front door.

"Who could that be?" she asked.

Sammy scrunched up his face and lifted his hands in that adorable way young children have. "Dunno."

"Shall we see?"

"'Kay.'' He wasn't interested in much except going to bed.

As Rowena headed for the door, she kissed his temple. "Are you going to stay awake long enough for a bath, Sammy-Jammy?"

With a sigh, he laid his head on her shoulder. "Dunno."

She chuckled softly and opened the door to find Jake's brother. "Oh. Mr. Stanbury. I thought you were already here."

Luke smiled. "Did they start without me?"

"Come in." She opened the door wide. "Actually, I think they finished without you. I saw Mrs. Hanson leave a few minutes ago."

Luke stepped through the door. "That frumpy old thing I passed on the path?" He patted Sammy on the back. "Hey, there, Mr. Sam."

"Hi," Sammy returned without much enthusiasm. He buried his face in Rowena's neck.

She tried not to frown as she closed the door. "Mrs. Hanson may not be much to look at, but she's an excellent cook—which you'd have discovered if you'd been here in time for dinner."

With one step, Luke was invading her space. He reached

out for a strand of hair that had escaped her clip. "You could serve me dinner."

His voice was low and intimate, as was the gesture.

Rowena had to keep herself from stepping back, which surprised her. She usually reacted to such blatantly sexual overtures by flirting...then flitting away.

After Heinrich, she'd discovered that the best way to protect her heart was to avoid intimacy. And the best way to avoid intimacy was to react to such suggestions with light banter, acting as if the man wasn't serious...but that she'd love it if he were. Most of the time, the man was so flattered that he didn't notice she'd fluttered away until she was gone.

Suddenly, however, even such harmless teasing seemed as if it would be a betrayal....

But to whom?

Jake's face popped into her mind.

No. She couldn't go there. She and Jake were not connected in any way. She was free to flirt with whomever she wanted to flirt with.

"Did the meal include any...whipped cream?"

His tone was so suggestive, Rowena wanted to cover Sammy's ears. She definitely did not want to flirt with Luke Stanbury.

"I don't know." So if she didn't want to flirt, how did she protect herself without offending a guest of the royal family? Her flirting method had worked so well for so long, she felt paralyzed.

"Too bad I don't have any kids," Luke said, drawing a finger across Sammy's back and down Rowena's arm. "You could come work for me."

Sammy shivered.

"I'm very happy where I am, thank you."

"So my brother is...treating you right?"

Rowena's eyes narrowed. Being suggestive to her was one thing. She was used to that. But she wouldn't stand by and let Luke denigrate Jake in any way. "*Your brother* has been a perfect gentleman."

Sammy must've felt her disquiet, because he reached back and pushed his uncle away. "Leave my Mommy alone."

"Your Mommy?" Luke grinned. "Is there something I should know?"

"Yes." Jake's voice boomed down the hall.

They turned to see him striding from the library, his face tight and even darker than usual.

Rowena felt like a damsel who was suddenly no longer in distress…because her knight had arrived.

Jake took Sammy from her arms and When she turned to leave, he grabbed her hand and held her at his side. "What you should know is that you're too late for dinner."

With her hand held firmly in Jake's, Rowena again felt like the damsel with her knight…protected and cherished.

But that was an illusion. An unfortunate holdover from the steady diet of fairy tales she'd grown up on. Damsels in distress lived happily ever after with the knights who rescued them.

But Rowena's happily ever after existed only in some storyteller's imagination.

As Luke passed a speculative glance between her and Jake, Rowena held her head high. They stood so close together, she knew the three of them appeared to be a family.

That was an illusion, too. They were not one…and never would be, no matter what Sammy said.

"Oh well." Luke grinned easily. "If you're not going to offer me anything, I guess I'll have to see if I can find a restaurant open."

Rowena tried again to pull her hand from Jake's. "I can warm up the—"

"Yes, why don't you do that?" Jake cut off her suggestion and kept her hand firmly in his.

Luke nodded. "Is Dad still here?"

"He left ten minutes ago."

Luke lifted an expressive brow at his brother, then let himself out the door.

"I'm sure there's plenty of leftovers," Rowena said. "I could've—"

"No, you couldn't have."

"But I don't mind—"

"You're not his servant. And you're not mine."

"But I—"

"I'm taking Sammy to bed." He leaned down and kissed her, then squeezed her hand and finally let go.

Shocked by the kiss, it took a moment for Rowena to realize he was heading for the stairs. "You don't want me to—?"

"No."

She frowned at his back. "What am I supposed to do?"

"I don't know. Relax."

"Sammy needs a bath," she called as he turned on the landing.

"He's already asleep. He can do without a bath for one night."

"But—"

"For God's sake, Ena." Jake leaned over the railing and looked down at her. "Don't you ever take a night off?"

She lifted her hands. "If I do, I spend it with my father."

"Cooking or cleaning or shopping for him, no doubt."

She frowned. "Usually."

Jake shook his head in apparent disgust. "Well, if you can't find something to do that isn't work, go in the library. I'll show you how to play."

She shivered, though his tone hadn't been at all suggestive. Funny how hearing something suggestive from one man was repulsive, and hearing something benign from another was suggestive.

"Play…" She cleared her throat. It was only in her mind. "What?"

"Chess, of course." He grinned. "Or did you have something else in mind?"

Lord help her, he was reading it. "Uh…no."

"I'll be there in a minute, then."

"Okay." She turned toward the library, telling herself she was not disappointed.

Jake slammed the phone on Annette's goodbye. She'd called to tell him her fiancé's lawyers had started the extradition order through the courts.

Jake threw back his chair and strode over to the window.

After three days of searching every family law database he could access, Jake had not come up with a single precedent strong enough to help him keep Sammy.

Not in United States' law, or Edenbourg's.

What the hell was he going to do? Meekly hand Sammy over to a woman who would stuff him in boarding school the moment he was old enough?

Never.

His father's words floated back to him.

So…you get married.

In the past few days, Jake had examined every angle of his father's suggestion, and he had to admit he could see its merits.

He would be just as married as Annette. And if he married quickly—within the next two weeks—he'd beat Annette to the altar. So he would be married before his ex-wife. Her whole case would fall apart.

Plus, he would have Rowena…in his bed…in his life.

Jake frowned.

He wanted Rowena. That much was certain. The only question was whether he was marrying her just to have her in his bed.

That's what had happened with Annette. He'd been so blinded by her beauty that he'd failed to noticed her loveliness was just skin-deep. She didn't have a motherly bone in her body.

But Rowena did.

Rowena was nothing like Annette. He was convinced of that now. He'd lived with her almost three weeks, and he'd seen her inner beauty. She was extremely protective of those she loved—such as Isabel and Sammy—and fiercely loyal.

He remembered the scene three days earlier between Rowena and Luke. She'd been the meek little servant with his brother until Luke had said something off-color about him…then she'd risen to his defense.

Did she love him?

The possibility made Jake's head swim, and he pressed it against the cool glass.

His mother had been more like Annette than Rowena…beautiful, but indifferent and quickly annoyed with him. But he'd loved her, and that's how he'd made the mistake of marrying Annette.

He wasn't going to make the same mistake twice. Since he had to have a wife, this time he was going to marry someone as different from Annette as he could get.

That woman was Rowena.

She'd make the perfect mother for Sammy…and the perfect wife for him.

No, he wasn't marrying Rowena just to get her in bed, though that was definitely a perk. He was marrying her for Sammy…and for her sweet nature…and her amazing loyalty…and her beautiful smile.

Now all he had to do was think of a reason why she should marry him.

The phone on the kitchen wall rang just when the cookie batter had formed a ball.

"Who could that be?" Rowena muttered.

"Dunno." From his perch on the counter, Sammy peered into the bowl as she turned off the mixer. "Cookies done?"

"Not quite." She unplugged the mixer and with a hand on Sammy's knee, grabbed the phone on the third ring. "Dowager Cottage."

"Rowena?"

"Isabel!" She hadn't heard from the princess since yesterday, when she'd left for New York. "Where are you?"

"I just left Jake's apartment."

Isabel's breathless voice let Rowena know how much the princess enjoyed her spying task. "And?"

"You're not going to believe what I found."

Rowena's heart sank. "What?"

Feeling a tug on her hand, she glanced over to see Sammy leaning to scoop a fingerful of cookie dough from the bowl. He grinned at her as he popped it into his mouth.

She was going to have to watch what she said.

"He has a stockpile of books on Edenbourg. A ton of them on the royal family. There were books there that I didn't even know existed."

"Is that all?"

"Is that *all?*" A horn blared in the background. "Why would he have books on the royal family? There must've been twenty-five."

"It's his family, too, you know."

There was a pause on the other end of the line. "You sound as if you're beginning to think he's not guilty."

Rowena smiled at Sammy as he stole a chocolate chip, hoping it didn't look as fake as it felt. She took a deep breath. "I don't think he is."

"Why? Have you found something?"

"No. I just..." Rowena felt split in two. She'd been friends with Isabel for so many years and had only known Jake for a few weeks. So why couldn't she bring herself to tell Isabel about the agreement she'd made with Jake? "I don't know. I just don't think he is."

"You're falling for him, aren't you?"

"No, Isabel, I'm—"

"Don't lie to me. I've seen how you watch him when you think no one's looking. Have you slept with him yet?"

"Isabel!"

"It's a valid question. If you're sleeping with the enemy, I'll have to take you out of his house."

"No, I'm not. I'm not planning on it, either. And I'm not leaving because Sammy—who's sitting right here—needs me."

Sammy's wide eyes glanced up from the cookie dough. "You leaving?"

Rowena smiled and with her forefinger, wiped dough off Sammy's nose. "No, Sammy-Jammy, I'm not."

"Edenbourg needs you, too, Rowena."

Rowena closed her eyes in guilt. "I know. But we're looking in the wrong direction, Isabel. I'm sure of it."

"How sure, Rowena?" Isabel demanded. "Sure enough to bet my brother's life on it? Because if whoever kidnapped my father wants the throne, then Nicholas is next."

Rowena hesitated. Did she feel sure enough of Jake's innocence? Nicholas was as dear to her as her own brother. "Yes. I'm as sure of his innocence as I am of my own."

Again there was a pause, then Isabel said, "Well, after you warned me off that crown prince who we later discovered was sleeping with his valet, I've learned to trust your judgment about people. So I have to believe you." She sighed. "I just wonder what Jake was doing with all those books. And why does he have a copy of the Treatise of Edenbourg?"

"I'm sure we'll know eventually. You weren't recognized, were you?"

"Not by a single soul." Isabel's voice was definitely

pleased. "And I took a cab both ways. Don't worry. Everything is fine. I'll be home tomorrow."

Rowena said goodbye and replaced the phone.

Why did Jake have all those books? For the same reason he had the Treatise? *Genealogical curiosity?* Did she believe that?

"Ena, guess what?"

Her name brought Rowena's attention back to her charge. He looked worried. "What, Sammy?"

"What's in'cence mean?"

Her face relaxed into a smile, and she mussed his hair. "It means being a sweet little boy, just like you."

"You not leaving, right, Ena?"

She lifted him off the counter and hugged him close. "No, Sammy-Jammy, I'm not leaving you. I love you, my sweet, innocent little boy."

He sighed and wrapped his tiny arms around her neck. "I love you, too, Ena."

Tears sprang to Rowena's eyes as she hugged him tight. This was the first time she'd told Sammy that she loved him, because it was the first time she'd realized it.

She didn't just love him because he was a child and still believed in all the good things life can give, who still believed in happily ever after. She loved him as much as she would love a child of her own. She knew that because at that moment she knew she'd gladly lay down her life to save his.

Which brought up a whole new set of questions.

Was her belief in Jake's innocence due to her love for Sammy? What about her feelings for Jake? Did she think she loved him only because she wanted Sammy for her own?

And most difficult of all—how would she ever be able to let them leave Edenbourg...without her?

The sound of the washing machine led Jake back to the laundry room behind the kitchen. He opened the door to find

Rowena pulling one of his shirts from the dryer, a hanger in her other hand.

"What are you doing?"

She started and straightened with a snap, dropping them both. "Jake! You scared me. What are you doing home so early?"

"Answer my question first."

"I…" She glanced down guiltily. "Mrs. Hanson's mother is sick and she had to leave early, so I told her I'd finish—"

"How many times have I told you that you're not one of the servants?" He hated seeing her doing menial tasks. She should be treated like a princess…and he intended to see that she was.

"Yes, Jake, I am." She reached down to pick up the dropped shirt.

He stopped her hand before it could close on the pinpoint cotton. He forced her to straighten, then bent and scooped her into his arms.

"Jake!" Her arms wrapped around his neck and held on tight. "What in the world are you doing? Let me down."

He headed for the library. "I came home early because I have something to discuss with you, and I don't intend to do it in the laundry room."

"But your shirts will be impossible to iron if I don't—"

"Not your problem."

She sighed in disgust. "Did anyone ever tell you you're a hardheaded man?"

"Frequently. Where's Sammy?"

"Napping. I just put him down twenty minutes ago."

"Good. That will give us at least an hour." He pushed the library door open with his foot.

"For what?"

He set her down in front of the couch. "Sit here."

"Why? What's happened? Jake, tell me what you—"

He shut her up with a hard kiss.

She stiffened for a brief instant, then melted against him.

Jake wrapped his arms around her waist and urged her mouth open. He hadn't intended to start this with a kiss, but now he knew it was the best idea he'd had all day.

He didn't draw back until she moaned, and then only because if he didn't stop, she wouldn't.

She rested her forehead against his chin. "What are you doing?"

He chuckled. "I thought I was kissing you. But if you didn't realize it, I guess I wasn't doing it properly, so maybe we should try it again."

She threw her head back to glare up at him. "You know what I mean."

He searched her lovely face. He was tempted to pick her up again and carry her straight upstairs. If he did, he wouldn't come down again for days. "Sit down. Please."

"But—"

"Please, or I'll just start kissing you again."

Her gaze fell to his lips. "And that would be bad because...?"

He groaned. "Ena..."

"All right." She pulled away and sat. "What?"

How did he start? "Something's happened. Something about Sammy."

Just as he had thought it would, mentioning Sammy got her attention. "What?"

He sat on the couch beside her and told her about Annette's phone calls. He gave her all the legal explanations and laid out the implications.

With each word, Rowena's beautiful hazel eyes grew angrier, her spine stiffened a little more.

"She can't take Sammy away from m...you," she said when he finished. "I won't let her."

"I'm afraid that she can…and she fully intends to."

"No, Jake. We can't let her. What are we going to do?"

"Well… I do have a solution."

"Oh, I knew you would. You're so smart." Her smile was brilliant as she twisted on the couch to fully face him. "What is it? Can I help?"

"Well, yes, as a matter of fact, you can."

"I'll do anything, Jake."

"Anything?"

"Of course, I'll do anything."

"I'm glad to hear you say that." He took her hands in his. "Because I want you to marry me."

Chapter Eight

"Marry you?" Rowena stared at Jake in shock.

This was every little-girl fantasy and every adult nightmare she'd ever had, rolled into one. The prince was offering marriage…happily ever after. But years too late. Years after she'd discovered that happily ever after was just as fictional as the fairy tales that touted them.

"Yes."

"Are you out of your mind? Or am I out of mine… hearing things?" She tried to pull her hands from Jake's, but he wouldn't let go.

"We're both totally sane," he assured her. "And I'm totally serious."

"No, Jake. It's impossible."

"Why?"

"Why?" Rowena felt as if she were in some crazy dream. "Well, aside from the fact that you're deranged is the fact that you're a prince and I'm as common as oxygen."

"Don't." A thundercloud passed over his face. "You are *not* common. Far from it. You're the most uncommon woman I know."

"Jake…"

"And I'm not a prince. I'm a very common, very untitled American, and no one can tell me who I can and can't marry."

"No matter what you say, you can't change the fact that you're fourth in line to the throne. And since you have a copy of the Edenbourg Treatise, you know that makes you a prince." She glared at him. "I'm a lady-in-waiting, Jake. Which is nothing but a glorified maid."

"I'm a lawyer. We're both in service occupations. But what does that have to do with anything?"

"*I* have to earn a paycheck."

"Which is one thing I want to stop. You're nobody's servant, Ena. I hate seeing you fetching and carrying and doing for everyone and their brother." He brought her hands to his lips and kissed them both in the middle of her palms. "You deserve to be treated like a princess…and I want the chance to see that you are."

Rowena shivered, as much from his words as from the gentle caress on the most sensitive part of her hands. For as long as she could remember, she'd dreamed about the handsome prince who would rescue her from a life of drudgery. He'd sweep her off her feet, carry her to his castle and *treat her like a princess*.

"Don't, Jake." She swallowed her emotion. "Don't say things like that."

"Why not?"

"Because I might believe you."

"You can believe every word." He smiled. "Marry me."

"But…we're not in love."

His smile faded. "Perhaps not, but I want you, and you want me."

So it boiled down to sex…again. What was the difference between Jake and Heinrich? Neither offered love. Neither promised her happily ever after.

She'd been right all along...every prince was the same.

"No." She finally pulled her hands from his and rose.

"Are you saying you don't want me?" He stood with a tiny, knowing smile as she backed two paces away. "Liar."

She winced. "I didn't say I didn't want you. But that's no reason to get married. If all you want is sex, then we can go upstairs right now and—"

"No."

"That's your favorite word, isn't it?"

His strong hands covered her shoulders. "This is not about sex, Ena. If that part bothers you, then we can keep things on a platonic level...until you get comfortable with it.. with me."

"What if I never do?"

He squeezed her shoulders. "I don't see that happening, do you?"

He was so smug, she broke his hold and stepped back. "It isn't the sex part that bothers me...." She was proud of herself for not flinching at the lie. "It's the marriage part."

"Why? I can provide for you. We can draw up an agreement. I'll put a certain amount of money in an account in your name. You can do whatever you want...."

Rowena's outrage must've shown on her face, because Jake trailed off. "What?"

"Do you think I can be bribed into marrying you?" Her words were as stiff as her spine.

"It's not bribery. It's the business of marriage."

"The *business* of marriage?"

He ran a hand through his hair. "I've been through this. It's better if certain things are spelled out beforehand. Expectations, duties, a contingency plan, that kind of thing."

"Spoken like a lawyer."

He lifted one brow. "That's what I am."

"Yes, it is, isn't it?" She crossed her hands over her stomach. "Tell me, what would my duties as your wife be?"

"Well, you'd pretty much do what you're doing now. Taking care of Sammy is the main task. I don't want you doing menial work of any kind, that's for sure."

"None? Ever?"

"No."

"What if you're hungry in the middle of the night and the cook has left the house? Will I be allowed to make you a sandwich?"

"I can make my own damn sandwich. And I can send my shirts to the laundry. And I can polish my own shoes. What's so wrong with not wanting my wife to work?"

"It's boring on my part, and archaic on yours. I happen to like taking care of the people I love. I like cooking. I like ironing. Perhaps not all day every day, but now and then. That's life, Jake. That's what marriage is…doing things for each other. Sharing things."

"But I don't like it when you—"

"Who asked you to? I know you think my job is demeaning, but I happen to enjoy it. Yes, I have to do menial work sometimes, but there's enough variety to keep life interesting. And sometimes it can be therapeutic to clean toilets."

He looked horrified. "You clean toilets?"

"No, not at the palace. But I had to when I lived at home. My father cleaned them, too. Are you saying you've never cleaned a toilet or changed a tire or ironed a shirt?"

"Of course I have," he admitted, but grudgingly. "All right, point taken."

He looked so disgruntled, Rowena relented. "It's not that I wouldn't enjoy being treated like a princess. But standing on a pedestal twenty-four hours a day can be exhausting. I know. I work for a real princess."

He stepped closer and lowered his voice. "How do you want to be treated?"

Though his sexy tone shimmied right to the core of her being, she stepped back. "Like a woman. That's what I am."

Suddenly his blue eyes caught fire. "I know."

"Oh, Jake." With one look, he could wash away all her defenses. To shore them up, she turned and walked to the window overlooking the sea. "It won't work."

He followed. "Yes, it will…if we make it work."

She remembered him talking about working hard to create happily ever after for Sammy. And she'd seen him keeping his word. He spent a lot of time with Sammy. He played with him, worked with him, disciplined him and loved him

The thought was oh so seductive— that Jake would put as much effort into making her happy.

"The first thing we do is work on the pre-nup. You can make any stipulations you want."

The walls that had been crumbling snapped back into place. "And how much money will you give me?"

He hesitated, probably because of her cold tone. "How much do you want?"

She twisted to glare up at him. "If you think you can make me happy with money, you don't know anything about me. You certainly don't know me well enough to marry me."

"What do you want?"

Love.

The word popped into Rowena's head, and she quickly turned her eyes back to the sea so he wouldn't see what she'd suddenly discovered buried deep within her heart.

She loved him. This royal prince.

No. Oh, no. God help her.

He stepped close and took her shoulders in his strong hands.

She let him draw her back against his warm, hard chest.

"What do you want, my sweet Ena?" His warm, whispered breath tickled her ear. "I'll give you anything. Jewels. Furs. Houses all over the world."

She closed her eyes to fight the tears. "Payment for taking care of your son, which I do anyway?"

"You need some compensation."

"Is this how you proposed to Annette? Was your marriage to her a business arrangement as well? No wonder it didn't last."

Jake frowned into Rowena's silky, fragrant hair as her words hit a chord of truth deep inside him. Could it be true? Was his marriage to Annette just a business...merger for lack of a better term?

He'd never thought about it that way, but now he realized it probably was true. Mergers and acquisitions had been his special talent in his practice...and were what he'd grown up with.

He was eight when his parents split. They even split up their children. Edward kept Luke and his mother kept him. He loved his mother, but as he grew up, she complained bitterly about not getting enough support from Edward.

What his parents had was a business merger gone bad. He'd never put it in those terms before, but now he realized he'd thought of it that way ever since finding out what mergers were.

Was that why he specialized in that area of law? To make certain the mergers he worked on would stand the test of time? Would stay together?

He suddenly realized that's what he'd been trying to do all his life—fix his parents' "merger." But he couldn't. Look at what he'd done with his own marriage. He'd made a ton of money for Annette, and expected her love and gratitude in return. Why was he so surprised when he didn't get it?

He couldn't do the same thing this time. He couldn't make the same mistake.

But if he was going to have any chance at all of keeping Sammy, he had to have a wife.

And he wanted Rowena. But if not with money, how did he convince her?

"All right. No pre-nup." He felt as if he was free falling.

"Jake…"

"Share your life with me, Ena. Let's share Sammy's. He needs a mother. He needs you."

Her breath broke on a sob. "You certainly know which buttons to push, don't you?"

"No. I just know that I have to have a wife in order to keep Sammy. And I don't want anyone but you."

She was silent for a long moment, then she turned to face him. Her face was far from happy. "All right, Jake. I'll marry you…for Sammy. But it will be in name only. At least until we get to know each other better."

Even with her conditions, relief washed through him. "I understand."

"I mean it. I won't sleep with a man I don't love…and who doesn't love me."

"I—"

"Don't you dare tell me you love me. You don't, or you wouldn't have proposed this way."

He nodded and pulled her closer. "All right, then. But I will tell you that I'm going to spend all my time and effort to make you love me."

She shivered in his arms. "When?"

"As soon as possible. I don't suppose tomorrow—"

"No. Absolutely not. Isabel is going to want a little fuss."

"And what do you want?"

"Right now…" her gaze fell to his lips "…I want you to kiss me."

He obliged. Fervently.

She sighed when he drew back.

"One more thing," he said.

Her dark golden eyes opened, but barely. "Hmm?"

"We can't tell anyone why we're getting married. If the judge residing over the extradition thinks I grabbed the first wife I could find, Annette will win anyway. He'll rule our marriage unstable, because we're not in love."

She frowned. "Which is true."

He shook his head. "We'll make it stable."

She sighed. "All right."

"Do you think you could act as though you love me, just a little bit?"

Her mouth twisted, but didn't come anywhere close to a smile. "Oh, I think I *might* be able to manage that."

"No, you're not."

"Yes, Isabel. I'm going to marry Jake."

Isabel's green eyes turned murky. "I knew it. You lied to me on the phone. You're in love with him."

Rowena looked down at her clasped hands, away from Isabel's accusing eyes. "Yes."

It was the first time she'd admitted it to anyone but herself. The first time she'd said the words out loud.

It felt right...and scared her more than jumping off a parapet of the palace's medieval wall.

"This is rather sudden, isn't it?" Isabel asked.

"Yes, I guess it is." Rowena felt disloyal, not telling Isabel the reason for the quick wedding, but even Isabel needed to believe the marriage was sincere. "We didn't see any reason to wait."

"Not even a week? Two?"

Rowena lifted her shoulder. "Why?"

"To give me time to plan something nice."

"To give you time to talk me out of it, you mean."

Isabel leaned forward and took Rowena's hand. "Are you sure you know what you're doing? You might think you're in love, Rowena, but you thought you were in love once before. You never did tell me what happened to make Heinrich leave so suddenly and never come back. I've heard things, but…''

Rowena ignored Isabel's not-too-subtle hint. She'd never been able to tell anyone about the humiliating experience with Heinrich. Not even her best friend.

Now she was marrying another prince. Would Jake see her the way Heinrich did? Common and frigid?

That fear, as much as anything, was why she refused to have a real marriage with Jake.

Her voice was shaky as she said, ''Of course I'm sure. I…love Jake. And I love Sammy. What more could I want?''

Isabel searched her face for a long, long moment. ''All right, Rowena. You're my best friend, so I have to believe you.'' Her eyes teared. ''I guess part of my fear is because I hate to lose you.''

Rowena began to cry, too, and reached for Isabel. ''You're not losing me. I'm getting married, that's all. I'll still be around, though he's not going to let me continue as your lady-in-waiting. But you'll be doing the same thing one of these days.''

''Yes, but will I love him the way you love Jake?''

''Of course you will.''

Isabel sighed. ''I wish you happily ever after, Rowena.''

Rowena hugged her friend tighter, so that Isabel couldn't see the fear in her eyes.

''Don't look so frightened,'' Jake whispered as he took her hand at the altar of the royal chapel.

Their families surrounded them. Sammy stood right beside them, his small hands bearing a pillow with hastily purchased rings. Rowena's father sat in the front pew beside Queen Josephine. Members of the royal family, including Luke, were scattered across the first two rows.

Isabel stood up with Rowena as her maid of honor. Jake's father served as his best man.

Jake squeezed her hand. "Brides are supposed to be happy, remember?"

Rowena curved her lips. "Is this better?"

Jake grimaced. "No."

"Dearly beloved…"

They turned to face the priest.

Despite the weight of her mother's silk shantung wedding gown, Rowena shivered in the coolness of the stone chapel, renowned for its marble angels. She felt their cold, lifeless eyes boring into her, accusing her of marrying this man under false pretenses…a man she knew didn't love her.

But I have my reasons, Rowena's mind whispered to the angels.

Though she didn't believe in happily ever after, Jake did. Perhaps if she was with him long enough, she'd start believing in it again, too, as she had when she was a little girl—the years she believed were the happiest of her life.

She wanted to be a part of Jake's happily ever after. And Sammy's, too.

If only she could forget that Jake didn't love her. If only she could forget that she was as guilty of lies and betrayal as his first wife, whom he now despised for those very reasons.

Even though she'd agreed to work hand-in-hand with Jake, even though she'd said she would share with him all information about the investigation that she came across, Rowena hadn't told him about the key she'd stolen so Isabel could search his apartment, or about what she'd found.

Even though Rowena believed with all her heart that Jake was innocent, she hadn't been able to convince anyone else. And she hadn't told him that, either. In fact, she'd told him that Isabel was on their side, but that was only true in a limited sense.

"...to love, honor and cherish..."

Jake's strong, deep voice echoed down the stone walls, broken by marble angels and arched columns. He sounded so convincing.

Even Isabel had admitted in the last two days that he seemed very much in love. When he was close by, he was never far from Rowena, touching her, holding her hand. He was solicitous of her welfare, and adamantly against her running errands, glaring at anyone who suggested it until they backed down.

In contrast, Rowena's vows, when she repeated them, hid in the corners of the sanctuary.

Jake slipped a heavy, diamond-studded ring on her finger, then lifted her veil and kissed her.

Happily ever after had begun.

Chapter Nine

Jake turned when a strong hand squeezed his shoulder. He immediately inclined his head in a bow. "King Nicholas."

"Please. I'm not king yet. Call me Nicholas. We're cousins, after all."

"If you wish."

The acting king inclined his head toward the French doors leading to the terrace. "I'd like a word with you, if you have a moment."

Jake nodded again. "Certainly."

Nicholas nodded to the ambassadors Jake had been speaking with. "If you gentlemen will excuse us...?"

The French and German delegates bowed from the waist as Nicholas turned toward the terrace. "I haven't really spoken to you one on one, Jake. I think it's about time two cousins became acquainted, don't you think?"

Jake kept his face blank as he followed the crown prince through the French doors. "I know you've been extremely busy, having to assume all the duties of the king and looking for your father, as well."

The April sunlight was weak as they stepped outside, barely overcoming the chill of the slight breeze drifting off the sea.

"That's no excuse. And it's not the reason." Nicholas walked casually across the terrace. "The truth is, I didn't want to know someone who, it seemed, might've killed my father."

Jake was surprised by his cousin's bluntness. Nicholas was a consummate statesman, always saying exactly the right thing. "So what has changed?"

Nicholas paused at the top of the steps leading to the garden and met Jake's gaze squarely. "I don't think you did it."

Jake's brow rose. "What changed your mind?"

Nicholas nodded toward the small lake.

Jake turned his head to see his wife strolling along the water's edge with Princess Rebecca. They'd just paused for Rowena to take Nicholas's daughter from the princess's arms.

Jake smiled. He could see the maternal look on Rowena's lovely face, even from a football field away.

"That's what changed my mind."

Jake returned his attention to the prince. "My marrying Rowena?"

"No. The way you smile every time you see her." Nicholas slapped Jake on the back. "My dear American cousin, I think we have more in common than genes. We both fell suddenly and desperately in love with very beautiful, very wonderful women. I believe a man who can love a woman so deeply could not harm a mouse, much less a king."

Again his cousin surprised him. Jake glanced back at the women to hide his confusion. *A man who can love a woman so deeply...* Was he that good an actor, or had Nicholas seen something Jake refused to admit...even to himself?

Nicholas extended a hand toward their wives. "Shall we join them?"

"I guess if the head of state can play hooky, I can, too."

Rowena was the first wife to notice their approach. She looked up from the infant in her arms, and her face lifted with a welcoming smile.

At that moment, Jake's confusion dissipated. Whether he was in love or not, he knew he'd made the right choice. He would never tire of seeing Rowena's hazel eyes lighting up to pure gold whenever he joined her.

When Rowena touched Rebecca's arm, the princess turned from the lake to bestow a similar smile on her own husband.

When they reached their wives, Jake slipped an arm around Rowena's tiny waist and leaned down to kiss her.

"Hi, beautiful." His smile felt as wide as sunshine.

Her face brightened even more. The proof of her happiness took his breath away. "Hi. What happened to your meeting?"

Nicholas answered for him. "We decided two ravishing women were infinitely better company than a roomful of European ambassadors."

"Ravishing?" Rebecca asked.

The prince gave his wife an evil smile. "Wasn't that what you did to me last night?"

Rebecca slapped his chest playfully. "Nicholas!"

"They're more newly married than we are, my love." Nicholas turned his smile on Rowena. "I'm sure Rowena did some ravishing of her own."

Rowena's cheeks flamed.

To save her, Jake switched to a more benign topic. "Where's Sammy?"

Rowena shifted the baby in her arms. "He's inside with the queen and Isabel. They insisted on reading him a story and putting him down for his nap. So Princess Rebecca and I decided to take the air."

"How many times do I have to tell you, Rowena? Drop the Princess. I have too many people using the formal address." Rebecca leaned against her husband as she gave Rowena a mock-stern expression. "You're part of the family now. You have no excuse."

Rowena's chin lifted. "Yes, I do. I was only a lady-in-waiting until three days ago."

"Give it up. We all know you're just as close to Isabel as a sister. And though you're still not her sister, you're her cousin. Most of the time, that's better. Sisters fight too much."

Jake leaned close to Rowena. "See? You're going to have to let go of the servant defense one of these days."

She gave him a look that was all but sticking out her tongue. "Not if I don't want to."

He grinned. "You keep insisting I'm a prince. That makes you a princess, not a servant. You can't have it both ways."

"Well, this *princess* needs to take a certain other princess in to change her diaper. If Rebecca and Nicholas will excuse me, I'll go."

Rebecca started forward. "I can—"

Rowena's pique melted into a smile. "No. Enjoy a few minutes alone with Nicholas. You get so few of them these days. Besides, I *want* to change her."

The crown prince and princess smiled at Rowena for understanding, then smiled at each other, and headed toward an arbor swing hidden from all but one path.

Rowena turned, and Jake turned with her.

"You don't need to get back to your meeting?" she asked.

"Not until Nicholas does, and it looks as if he might be a while."

"Yes, it does." Rowena sighed dreamily. "They're very much in love. Nicholas made a good choice when he picked Princess Rebecca for his wife."

"Just Rebecca," he corrected.

She didn't even frown at him. "Anyway, it was as good a choice for the country as it was for him. She's going to be an excellent queen."

Jake's attention was caught by a group of gardeners working in a flower bed on the next path. There was something wrong about the three. They were so clumsy at what they were doing, and they kept looking over their shoulders.

"Jake? Why are you stopping? This is a stinky diaper and I need to get it changed before LeAnn's skin gets irritated."

"Go on, sweetheart," he said distractedly. "I'll be there in a—"

Suddenly he knew what was wrong. All three men had bulges under their shirts, right where a shoulder holster would be.

"Jake? What's—"

"Go." He placed a hand in the middle of Rowena's narrow back and shoved her in the direction of the palace. "Now."

She turned back. "But—"

The three dropped their shovels and turned toward the isolated arbor hiding the man next in line for the throne.

"*Now*, Ena. Take the princess and go!"

She must've seen the men then, too, because her face blanched. "Oh my God. Jake, no! You'll be hurt. I'll call the palace guard. They—"

"There isn't time." He turned her toward the palace again. "Go. Now. Whatever happens to them, you have to save their daughter."

"Be careful!" she threw over her shoulder as she held the baby tighter and ran down the path.

Relieved to have her heading toward safety, Jake turned and sprinted down the path in the opposite direction.

How the hell did these goons make it past the Spandex-tight security at the palace? And how the hell was he going to stop them? They were armed, they looked like they knew how to use their guns and they were three against his one.

Jake skidded to a halt as he rounded a tight copse of elm. Their backs to him, the men were just surprising the royal couple. Two men had their guns out. The third had a rope in his hand.

With the odds, Jake needed the element of surprise. It was his only weapon.

Instead of continuing down the path, he threaded his way through the elms as silently as he could.

From between trees, he saw Nicholas stand, trying to position himself in front of Rebecca. In his most authoritative voice, the prince demanded an explanation for being disturbed.

One of the men ordered him in heavily accented English to turn around. From the sound of it, they were German.

But that could mean anything—from them being hired thugs to the possibility that a militant group of Germans were trying to take over Edenbourg. The last wasn't likely, but the island kingdom lay between the German shore and the British. Both had claimed it at one time or other during the last millennium, only to be beaten back by Edenbourg's small but well-maintained navy. Even during the Second World War, the Germans hadn't set a foot on Edenbourg soil.

Jake paused behind a large elm just a few feet behind the kidnappers. He had to attack before they succeeded in tying Nicholas, who was just being forced to turn by the man with the rope. With any luck, Nicholas would have the presence of mind to take down the man tying him when Jake pounced.

He crouched behind the tree, gathering strength. When the man on the left began to move toward the princess, Jake sprang with a loud yell.

He tackled the man about to grab the princess. The man

was burly, outweighing Jake by at least fifty pounds, but the element of surprise helped Jake take him to the ground.

As they went down, Jake made sure he landed on top. Even so, the gun struck him on the side of the face and fired.

A woman screamed. A man grunted.

But Jake couldn't look. He was too busy struggling to hold the husky German on the ground.

Just as Jake succeeded in forcing the gun from the man's hand, another shot fired. Jake felt a hot sting along the outside of his right thigh.

A muffled crack. An anguished scream. More harsh shouting in German from the man beneath him and the others.

Suddenly a blow to Jake's temple stunned him, giving his opponent the chance to throw Jake off and run.

Dazed, Jake still managed to roll to his knees in time to see all three disappear through the trees.

Then he turned to see Nicholas bending over Rebecca, his face twisted and hard.

Blood stained the side of her dress.

"I'm all right, sweetheart," she insisted.

"The hell you are." Nicholas tore off his jacket, then his shirt. "Where in God's name are the palace guards?"

As if to answer him, more shots sounded in the distance.

"I'll bring them." Jake shook his head to clear it and tried to stand. When he did, he stumbled on his right leg.

"You're not going anywhere on that, my friend," Nicholas said as he held his folded shirt to his wife's side. "Sit down. Help will be here any minute."

Jake tore his ripped pants leg so he could determine the damage. "It's just a flesh wound."

"But a deep one," Nicholas said. "That's why it's bleeding so much."

Jake copied Nicholas. He threw off his jacket and pulled off his shirt. Then he sat on the ground and tied his shirt around his thigh.

Just as he finished bandaging it, palace guards surrounded them. Two of them roughly hauled Jake to his feet.

"Stop," Nicholas bellowed. "Take your hands off this man. He's the one who saved us."

Just noticing what his men were doing, the captain shoved them away from Jake. "Didn't you hear the shots near the wall? The perpetrators are over there." He turned and bowed to Nicholas. "Sorry, Your Highness. They're new."

Nicholas waved his explanation away and returned his attention to Rebecca as another guard barked into a radio for emergency medical help.

Still dazed, Jake watched the others sweep the area. Then he felt a touch on his arm.

"Come and sit on the swing by Rebecca," Nicholas said. "You don't look too steady on your feet."

Jake lifted a sore shoulder. "I'll live."

The prince smiled grimly. "While I'll be eternally grateful for that, I'm sure I will never hear the end of it if I don't insist. Rebecca is adamant that you join her, and you know how difficult wives can be when they don't get their way."

Jake smiled. Even in times of crisis, Nicholas remained the consummate statesman, giving Jake an excuse to be weak. Even though he didn't need it—his head was already clearing—he relented. "All right...for Rebecca's sake."

Jake winced with all five steps it took him to reach the swing.

Rebecca smiled weakly as he sat and held out her hand for his. "Thank you, Jake."

"Was it my man's gun that got you?" he asked her.

She nodded.

"I'm sorry. I should've—"

"Don't be silly, Jake." She squeezed his hand. "You couldn't help it."

He lifted his head to Nicholas. "I'm afraid I didn't see what happened, other than what I was doing."

"When you so heroically attacked the biggest one, I took advantage of their disorder and threw myself against the one attempting to restrain me. He staggered back against the leader, then ran off. When the potshot the leader took at you didn't stop you, he struck you with his gun. Meanwhile, I grabbed a stone—thank God for landscaping—and cracked his arm with it."

Rebecca shivered. "I heard the bone break."

"Yes, I think it did. Anyway, your man jumped up, knocked me down and they took off together."

"Your men caught them, though, right?"

The prince's face turned grim. "Not yet. It seems as if they might've gotten away."

"How is that possible? This place has been locked up tighter than Fort Knox ever since I've been here."

"There's a door in the outside wall, put there as an escape route during medieval days. It's been boarded up for centuries, and mostly forgotten, but these men apparently knew about it."

"Damn. So whoever's behind all this trouble knows this place pretty well."

"Or at least knows someone who knows the palace well."

Nicholas and Jake met each other's gaze squarely. Without a word passing between them, they both recognized and acknowledged what they'd known before—both of them were innocent.

Two hours later, Rowena threw open the door to one of the countless spare bedrooms in the palace, barely recognizing and for once not caring that it banged back against a priceless antique side table.

"Jake."

He was propped up against a mound of pillows on the high four-poster bed, just removing the ice pack he'd been holding against his face.

"Oh, my God."

An ugly red and purple knot crawled from his right eye into his dark brown hair.

"Hi, sweetheart."

"Don't you sweetheart me."

She walked slowly to the end of the bed, assessing his injuries. Since he wasn't wearing a shirt, his chest was open for viewing and revealed several nasty bruises and cuts. His right leg lay outside the sheet pulled over him for modesty, letting her see the bandage the doctor had affixed to the gash in his leg.

She placed both hands on the foot rail for support, then leaned on them heavily. "You call this being careful?"

Jake lifted that quirky left eyebrow of his. "I'm alive."

"You were shot," she said, uncaring that her tone was accusatory.

"Are you angry with me? For saving the hide of your precious prince? The one you were willing to risk your own neck for?"

"Don't you dare get flippant with me! I've been insane with worry for two hours. When I reached the terrace I heard two gunshots. I wasn't told until half an hour ago that one of them didn't find your heart." Rowena knew she was being unreasonable, but when she'd heard those two shots, she'd felt as if they'd both found hers.

Jake finally had the good sense to look contrite. "I'm sorry, sweetheart. The EMTs—or whatever you call them over here—dragged me up to this room and the doctor started poking and prodding immediately. You know how doctors are…they won't listen to anything that's not a symptom until they at least stop the bleeding."

She gasped. "There was that much?"

He cursed under his breath and patted the bed. "Come here."

She shook her head. "You're hurt."

But oh, she wanted to. She needed to touch him—to be sure he was here, real, alive. She wanted to hold onto him and never again let him out of her sight.

"I'll be more hurt if you don't come." His hand beckoned. "A kiss will do me more good than anything."

Her eyes filled with tears, but she sat carefully on the left side of the bed. The bruises and cuts looked even worse up close. "Damn you, Jake Stanbury. Couldn't you have just distracted them or something?"

He pulled her down and tucked her along his left side. "It looked as if they were determined to either capture Nicholas or kill him."

Rowena gingerly rested her hand on his hard, flat stomach, trying to find a spot that wasn't injured. "So you decided to play the hero."

"There was no decision to it. They were in trouble, so I did what I could."

She raised her head to glare at him. "And almost got yourself killed doing it! It wasn't as if you were helping a poor old woman change her tire in the rain. Those men had guns...and you knew that before you followed them."

"I couldn't not help them, Ena. Surely you can understand that."

"What if you'd been killed? What would've happened to Sammy? And me?"

He pushed back an errant strand of her hair. "You know, you're making it sound as if you care."

Rowena hid her face against the soft hair on his chest. That was the problem...she cared too much. And the amount you care is in direct proportion to the potential harm the recipient of that caring can do to your heart. If she hadn't already suspected she was in love with him, she knew now. Damn ten times over.

"Of course I care. I'm your wife."

Naturally, he wasn't going to let her hide over a declaration like that. He placed an amazingly strong finger, swollen from punching something or someone, under her chin and made her look at him. "Wives usually care because they're in love with their husbands."

Now what was she supposed to say to that? "Do you want me to love you?"

"Yes."

She blinked.

"Why are you surprised?" he asked.

"Because…well…when we married, we said we weren't in love."

"You said that. I didn't."

"Oh. Hmmm. I see. So…" She swallowed hard, though it was difficult with his finger still under her chin. "So, do you love me?"

"No."

He said it so matter-of-factly, as if it didn't matter. As if it didn't crush her heart. "Yet you want me to love you?"

He kissed the tip of her nose. "Yes."

"Do you have any idea how much power that would give you over me? Do you know how much you could hurt me?"

Next he kissed her lips. "Don't worry, sweet Ena. I will treasure your heart as if it were the world's biggest, brightest, most perfect diamond."

Tears stung her eyes. "I don't believe you. Men, especially royal men, use women's love like a weapon against them."

He turned on the bed so he could gather her close. "Don't cry, sweetheart. If I could love you, I would. But after what Annette did to me, I don't think I have any love left in me."

"You love Sammy."

He kissed her temple softly. "That's different. Sammy is my son."

"I see." And she really did. Actually, his words gave her hope. She'd said the same thing after the Heinrich incident.

She'd been determined never to fall in love again... especially with a royal. But she had.

If she could do it, then perhaps he could, too.

"I want you, Ena," he whispered against her hair. "And I like you very much. You're the only woman I can see living the rest of my life with. I promise I'll be faithful. Isn't that enough?"

She drew back so she could see his face. "So this is a forever marriage?"

He looked taken aback. "I hope so. I'm going to work hard to see that it is. Didn't you hear the vows you gave me? 'Until death us do part.'"

"I didn't know. We never talked about that, really. I thought it might just be until Annette calls off her lawyers."

"No. It's the forever kind. Okay?"

She nodded. "All right."

"Promise?"

Her lips twisted. "Sounds as if I already did."

Another woman had promised forever to him, too. Instead, Annette had destroyed all the love Jake had to give. Annette. Rowena hadn't really thought much about the "other woman" before, but now she became determined to learn everything she could about Jake's ex-wife.

Maybe she could find a clue how to give Jake back his heart...so he could give it to her.

Chapter Ten

Two days later, Jake hid a velvet box behind his back when he entered the library in the middle of the afternoon. He'd come home during Sammy's nap time deliberately…to give something very special to his wife.

Rowena was on the phone at the desk and looked startled when she caught sight of him.

"I see. All right. Thank you. You've been an enormous help…. Yes, please call if you find anything else. Goodbye."

She replaced the receiver. "I thought you were going to be at the palace all day."

"The boss let me come home early." He grinned and walked around the desk. "You didn't need to hurry off the phone."

"I was finished." She leaned back in the chair so he could kiss her, which he did…thoroughly.

"My," she said when he finally let her lips go. "You *are* acting like a boy let out of school. Even looks as if you're hiding something. What is it? A frog you found in the pond?"

"So the princess can kiss it and turn it into a handsome prince? No, thank you. Don't need the competition."

"That's good. Because we're fresh out of real princesses in this house. You'll have to try the palace next door if you need any frogs kissed."

He drew her up from the chair and kissed her again. "You're a real princess. According to the Treatise of Edenbourg, that is. If you need to reference it, you'll find a copy in my—"

"I know where it is," she said, blushing. "I just keep forgetting."

"No, you don't. You want to keep thinking of yourself as someone's maid." He took her hand and led her across the room to the couch in front of the windows. "But you won't be able to anymore. You're about to feel like a princess."

"I am?"

"Well, I hope you like it."

"Like what?"

He sat and drew her onto his lap. When she was settled and looking at him expectantly, he couldn't resist kissing her again—deeply. In fact, he got so involved in kissing, he forgot about his gift until he laid Rowena back on the couch and the velvet box slid to the floor.

The sound startled them both back to reality.

"Damn. I forgot."

"What is it?"

He sat up and pulled her with him. Then he leaned over and retrieved the box. "This."

She frowned at the velvet and repeated, more suspiciously this time, "What is it?"

He smiled in anticipation. "Something to wear to the next palace event. I know you're nervous about attending one."

"Well, it'll be the first time I'll be at one as a Stanbury."

"And it will be the first time you'll be at one without a tray to hold in front of you like a shield."

She looked at him, startled. "What?"

He kissed the tip of her adorable nose. "Don't worry. Your secret is safe with me."

"What secret?"

"I saw the way you would carry a tray of something around the room, holding it like a shield to protect you from overly zealous men."

She regarded him like a zoologist encountering a species never before seen. "You noticed? No one's ever... I didn't think you even knew who I was then."

"You bet I noticed you. And I'll tell you another thing, every man in the room noticed you, too."

"But not like that. None of them knew I was trying to keep them from touching me." She shivered.

He wanted to ask why she had never talked to him, but refrained. He wanted her in a happy mood...a festive mood...a loving mood. "Well, you never have to carry a tray of anything again." He lifted her left hand and kissed her finger just above her wedding ring. "If this doesn't protect you, Mrs. Stanbury, Mr. Stanbury will."

She relaxed into a smile. "Which one? There are four of you."

"Oh, I think any of us will come to your rescue, because you're one of our princesses." He placed the velvet box in her hand. "And since you still can't quite believe it, this should make you feel like one."

She opened the box cautiously, as if afraid the frog they had talked about would jump out at her. When it was open, she gasped. "Amber. Oh my God, Jake, they're beautiful."

"Not half as beautiful as you," he said, proud that he'd pleased her.

"But..." She closed the lid on the necklace and earrings.

"You already bought me the designer gown, and it was so expensive."

"Don't worry about the money, sweet Ena. I have plenty. And it pleases me to spend it on you." He grinned. "Doesn't this buy me a kiss or something?"

She regarded him solemnly for a moment, then gathered her muscles to rise.

He wouldn't let her. "Hey, what's wrong?"

"You're trying to seduce me with jewelry and it won't work. I told you I'm not interested in your money. I'm not interested in looking like a princess…or feeling like one or smelling like one or even being one."

"You don't like amber?"

"You don't understand anything! The necklace and earrings are lovely. It's the reason you bought them I don't like."

"And that is…?"

"You're trying to buy my love."

Jake went still, stunned by her perception. This was the second time Rowena had seen straight into his soul, ferreting out aspects of his psyche he didn't even know were there…until she pointed them out.

Yes, he was trying to buy her love. Not knowing how to achieve his goal any other way, he fell back on what had worked with Annette.

"I want you to feel special." *Because of me.* But the excuse was only surface-deep, and was as flimsy as it sounded. "I saw these and knew they would match your eyes."

She seemed more disappointed in his answer than she'd been with his gift.

Fool. He'd already discovered that Rowena was nothing like his ex-wife. Why did he think this would work?

So…what would work?

He'd learned a long time ago it was best to go right to the source. "What do you want, Ena?"

Her beautiful eyes turned smoky. "What you really want to know is how to make me love you."

Her stark insight startled Jake.

He'd sat through countless negotiations, never giving a clue as to whether he was bluffing. His poker face was one reason he was so successful, and in high demand.

Yet this tiny woman saw past the surface to the man inside—a man so deeply buried even Jake didn't know him.

No one had ever done that before. No one had ever wanted to.

Until now.

The possibility that someone could know him so intimately was frightening…yet seductive at the same time. So seductive.

He had to find a way to keep this woman, a way to make her stay with him…forever.

His throat was raw with emotion. "Yes. Will you tell me?"

She frowned down at the velvet box for a long moment. Finally, hesitantly, she said, "Share yourself with me. Tell me your hopes and fears. Your plans for the future. What you want Sammy to be when he grows up." She twisted in his lap to fully face him. "All I want is you, Jake. Just you."

Then she kissed him. The kiss was just like her—sweet and passionate at the same time.

Jake responded with all the passion inside of him, though she'd scared him senseless.

He'd found what he wanted—a woman who wasn't impressed by titles or money. A woman who saw the man he was and would, he hoped, love him for being that man.

But she wanted something in return. Something he didn't know if he could give—himself.

When they came up for air, he brushed a strand of deep

red hair from her cheek. "How about if I take you and Sammy away tomorrow? Do you know some place we can have a picnic or something?"

"What about your leg?"

"As long as I don't have to march twenty miles, it'll be okay."

"Then a picnic would be lovely," she said on a sigh. "There's some ruins on the north side of the island. An old castle. We could explore around them and have a picnic on the heath."

He kissed her again, briefly. "It's a date, Mrs. Stanbury."

"I'll hold you to it, Mr. Stanbury." She smiled. "Or better yet, I'll tell Sammy when he wakes from his nap. He'll hold you to it, or you'll never hear the end of it."

"Don't worry. I'm not going to back out."

Perhaps the outing would be a reprieve, or perhaps he'd learn even more about himself... something that might give him a clue how to proceed.

He'd always skated by, showing women only what he wanted them to see. Now, in order to have Rowena the way he wanted her, he had to draw back the curtains of his soul...and show her what lay hidden behind them.

He didn't think he could do it.

Why not? a voice inside asked. *She's already seen your ugliest parts.*

Was it possible Rowena could know him—all of him—and still love him?

Perhaps. Perhaps not. There was no telling what else was hidden in the murky depths.

What seemed certain, however, was that she wouldn't love him unless he opened up. And he wanted...needed her love.

So he had to try.

Even though it was possible he would be damned either way.

* * *

Jake grabbed the extra blanket and tugged Rowena to her feet. "Let's sit by the edge of the cliff."

"But Sammy's napping."

"We won't be thirty yards away. We'll disturb his rest if we stay here talking."

"All right." She stooped and tucked Sammy's comfort blanket more tightly around his little body.

When she straightened, Jake offered his hand.

She took it with a smile, and they strolled hand-in-hand to the edge of the cliff.

The stitches in Jake's leg pulled as he walked, but he didn't favor it. The cushion of grass they walked through helped. Incredibly thick and green, it was interspersed with heather, the stalks of which were nearly knee-high and on the verge of blooming.

Up the hill to their right, the ruins of Methlick Castle rose from the side of the cliff. Nearly a third of its stones had tumbled into the sea, attesting to its abandonment due to cliff erosion.

"I haven't seen very much of Edenbourg, but I have to say you have a beautiful country. It's the kind of place you imagine as the setting for fairy tales."

"Which isn't necessarily a good thing."

"Why not?"

"Because you grow up believing in them."

He was distracted from her comment for a moment by sharing the task of spreading the blanket a few feet from the edge of the cliff. The heath grew right off the edge.

He sat on the blanket, angling so he had a view of the sea, the castle and the massive oak Sammy slept beneath. Rowena settled between his legs, leaning back against his chest. He wrapped his arms around her, and she rested her hands on them.

Her hair smelled of ocean breezes and sunshine, and he breathed the scent in deeply.

The sea was rough today, though the breeze blowing off it was warmed enough by the April sun not to be chilly. He could see a freighter in the distance, probably out of Hamburg. Otherwise, the horizon was broken only by skittish clouds.

"What's so bad about believing in fairy tales?" he asked.

Rowena sighed. "You don't let go of anything, do you?"

"I'm a lawyer, remember?"

"And a very good one, from what I hear."

"Thank you."

"That wasn't necessarily a compliment."

He could hear the smile in her voice. "More lawyer jokes? We were talking about fairy tales, as I recall."

She sighed again. "I grew up hearing fairy tales on a daily basis. My mother loved to tell them, and I loved to hear them. I always dreamed of growing up to be a princess. My prince would ride up on a shiny black horse and carry me off to live happily ever after in Methlick Castle. Refurbished, of course."

"I thought princes rode white horses in fairy tales."

"They usually do, but I prefer black ones."

"So your prince was a black knight, so to speak. I can see a trend here. You go for the bad boys. No wonder you married me. I'm a lawyer."

She chuckled. "Do you have a black steed?"

"I have a black BMW at home. Does that count?"

"I suppose it will have to, won't it?"

He kissed the top of her head. "So when did the fairy tales start falling apart? When you started dating?"

"No. Not until I met Prince Heinrich of Leuvendan."

She told him the story of how she'd fallen in love for the first time, and how her heart had been dashed to pieces when Heinrich insisted on her sleeping with him to prove her love.

When she wouldn't, he told everyone who'd listen that she'd performed all kinds of kinky sex acts with him.

As she talked, she relaxed against him. He, however, grew stiffer with every word. By the time she finished, he wanted to kill the man. No wonder she had such a low opinion of princes.

"So that's how you got your reputation," he said when she was finished.

"Yes. Memories are long in such a small country."

"I'm sorry, Ena. If you'll tell me where this Leuvendan is, I'll go beat him up for you."

She touched one of the bruises still showing on his arm. "You mean, now that you've had practice?"

"Who needs practice to beat up bullies? They usually run."

"There's no need. Last year he married Princess Malika from Sabinov. That's punishment enough for anybody."

"Know her well, do you?"

"She visited Edenbourg a few years ago. She was a classmate of Dominique's. She didn't bring a maid and I had to help her dress one night. After two hours with her, I threatened to quit if Isabel asked me to assist her again. Isabel found someone who needed the money desperately enough to put up with Malika for a few days. She was not invited back, thank God."

Jake tightened his hold. "I wish I'd been here then, to spare you."

Her head moved back and forth beneath his chin. "It's sweet of you to want to protect me from bad people, Jake, but not smart. If you're raising Sammy this way, it's got to stop."

"Why?"

"Because one day you won't be there when he runs into someone like that, and he won't know how to act. Better to let him experience the nastiness with you there to show him how to deal with such situations."

Emotions swept over Jake, so intense they made his head swim.

Rowena was a wise and patient mother…and that was just one of the many reasons he loved her.

Yes, he loved this bewitching little pixie of a woman, whose head barely reached his chin.

Relief washed over him, making him realize the effort it had taken to repress his feelings. He was such a fool. Loving Rowena felt good…felt right. He wasn't going to hide it any longer.

"Jake?"

"Hmmm?"

"Will you tell me about Annette?"

"Damn. Talk about spoiling the mood."

She sat up and faced him. "I know the basics. You were married over four years, then divorced nearly two years ago and you were awarded custody of Sammy. But I don't know the whys."

He took her hands in his and told her everything. He opened his marriage up with a can opener and showed her every dark place inside. He praised Rowena for her accurate assessment of his personality. He told her about every wrong turn he'd made and about every curve Annette had thrown him.

As he talked, Rowena listened, amazed with each revelation. Jake took the blame for a lot of what had gone wrong, even though Rowena had gathered enough information about Annette to know the woman's selfishness ran bone-deep.

And the more he talked, the more Rowena realized how much like Annette she was. Not so much for the betrayal of moving in to spy on him. That, after all, was for her country.

No, Rowena's selfishness went even deeper than Annette's. Annette didn't love Jake, so it was no surprise that she could do the things she did.

But Rowena loved him…and she was deliberately withholding that love. She refused to give him what he wanted…her body, her love, her heart. All because of some stupid notion that she was protecting herself. As if her heart would be less broken if she withheld the things he wanted…the things he needed so desperately from a woman…the things he'd never had.

No wonder he couldn't love her back.

The thought of giving her body to him frightened her breath away. But perhaps—if she had the courage to do it— if she showed Jake her love, one day he might love her in return. Just a little.

Shaking but determined, she knelt in front of him. With a hand on either side of his face, she stroked her fingers through his thick, dark hair. ''Thank you for sharing your pain with me.''

His eyes were intense. ''Thank you for listening.''

She took in a fortifying breath. ''Jake?''

''Yes?''

''I—''

Suddenly a movement past him caught her attention and all her mother instincts went on alert as her eyes riveted on Sammy.

What she saw, however, made her smile. ''Oh, my.''

''What is it?''

''Shh. Look.''

A giggle drifted across the heather as Jake slowly twisted from the waist. ''What the—? It won't hurt him, will it?''

''I don't think so,'' she whispered. ''Not if we don't startle it.''

A tiny fawn leaned over Sammy. Their son had turned on his back so he could reach up and stroke the fawn's delicate head.

As they watched, the fawn swiped its tongue across Sammy's cheek, making the boy giggle again.

"Where's the—? There she is." Jake nodded toward the castle.

The doe grazed about forty yards away, keeping a watchful eye on her offspring. Seconds later, her head came up. She gave a bleating call, which made the fawn back away from Sammy, then turn and bound away after its mother.

Sammy rolled over to his elbows and watched them go, wonder all over his face.

Jake snaked a hand around Rowena. "Thank you for bringing us here. This is truly a magical place."

Chapter Eleven

Exhausted and still full of wonder, Sammy fell asleep early that evening. Jake and Rowena put him to bed together.

"He didn't even want us to read him a story," Jake said softly as he closed Sammy's door. "That's a first."

Rowena waited two steps away, her arms wrapped tight around her waist. It was now or never.

When the door clicked, Jake turned to her. He searched her face. "I—"

"Can—"

They both chuckled nervously.

"You first," Jake said.

"Okay. I just..." She glanced down the hall. "Can we talk?"

"Certainly. Where do you want to go?"

"Oh, anywhere. How about..." She cleared her throat. "How about your bedroom?"

Rowena had never gone into Jake's bedroom with him in it, so this was new.

Jake's only comment on the difference, however, was a

lifting of his dark eyebrow. He placed a hand on the small of her back and guided her down the hall, as if she didn't know where the room was.

Rowena shivered at the heat of his hand resting on her so intimately.

"Are you cold?" he asked.

"No. I..." She shivered again. "No, I'm not cold."

The lamp beside his bed was the only light as they stepped into the master bedroom. This room was decorated in the ornate French style of Louis XV, all gold and gilt.

Jake closed the door behind him.

Rowena faced him. "I..."

After an expectant pause, he prompted, "Yes?"

"I..." She couldn't look at him and get through this, so she turned and walked slowly across the antique carpet. "I realized something today, while we were talking, and I thought I should tell you."

"All right."

She reached the Louis XV burled walnut and inlaid dressing table on the opposite wall and glanced in the mirror mounted over it. He hadn't moved.

"I've been very selfish, I realized. I've been withholding information you should have that—"

"Information about the king?" He took a step forward.

The king? What did the king have to do with— "Oh. No. Not that. I just..."

She looked down at the figurine her hands were toying with.

"For God's sake, Rowena, just spit it out."

She spun so suddenly, she had to grab onto the dressing table behind her back to keep from falling. "I love you."

Instead of the exultant joy she expected, he seemed surprised.

"Did you hear what I said? I said—"

"You love me." He finally smiled. "This is what you wanted to tell me?"

"Well, yes, isn't that enough?"

He covered the distance separating them and enfolded her in his arms. "Oh, yes, my sweet Ena. It's enough for a lifetime. As long as you intend it to last that long."

She clung to him. "I'm afraid you're going to have to put up with me forever. Because it's not going away."

He drew back and locked into her gaze. The look on his face was everything she could have hoped for—wonder and passion and relief and joy.

"How do you know it won't go away?"

"Because I tried to make it," she said. "But it won't, so you're stuck with it…with me."

He grinned. "I can think of worse things to be stuck with." His intense gaze swept over her face. "Much worse. What made you realize it?"

"Well…" She dropped her head guiltily. "I have a confession here…"

This time he didn't force her to look at him. He just said, "Don't hide from me, sweetheart."

Rowena bravely lifted her chin on her own.

His smile was as bright as the sun. "What's this confession?"

"I've known for a while."

"That you love me."

"Yes." She swallowed. "Since you proposed…and I suspected it before that. I didn't tell you because you told me you wouldn't love me back. But I realized today I was being selfish, and a coward. That isn't love, because it's conditional, and my love for you isn't."

She met his gaze squarely. "I love you, Jake Stanbury, for always…whether you love me back or not. And I want to be your wife in every sense of the word."

He sucked in a quick breath and rested his forehead against hers. "Ena. Sweetheart. Do you mean that?"

She slipped her arms around his neck. "Yes, my love, I do. Will you make love with me? Tonight?"

"And every night afterward…and every morning, too." He kissed her. "Until death us do part."

"Oh, Jake…"

He wrapped his arms around her tightly, as if he wanted to make her body a part of his. Then he pulled her onto her toes and kissed her until even they curled off the floor.

He lifted her then, all the way, and carried her to the bed.

When he set her on her feet beside it, she turned to climb on but he took her shoulders. "Wait. There's something we need to discuss while we still can."

"What?"

"Are you wanting to have children with me? The reason I'm asking now is I need to know if we should use protection."

She placed her hands on his broad, warm chest, and smiled when she felt the staccato beat of his heart. "Do you want more?"

"Yes. From what I've seen, most children benefit by having siblings, so I want more for Sammy. But I want more for myself, as well. I love kids." He gently squeezed her shoulders. "But it's up to you."

She stood on tiptoe and kissed his chin. "Then don't use protection. I want to have your baby."

An emotion swept over his face that she'd never seen—almost…ecstatic pain. His eyes closed tight, and he buried his face in her neck. "Oh, Ena, I can't wait to see you round and luscious with my baby inside you. Will you let me touch you? Will you share what you're going through…with me?"

She knew without him saying why her answer was so important. "Annette didn't, did she?"

He shook his head. "She hated being pregnant. I didn't

see her naked from the pregnancy test on. And I mean that literally. We never had sex again." He finally drew back and met her gaze. "I won't call it making love. I don't think it was ever that."

"Jake." She cupped his face in her hands, felt the rasp of a day's growth of beard against her palms, the hard line of his jaw against her fingers. She never knew a man this strong could be so vulnerable. She never knew a woman could have so much power to hurt him.

She wanted to have that much power...so she could prove to him that she'd never use it against him.

"Give me your child," she whispered. "I will never hold you away from it, even though it's in my body. Because it will be your child...your gift. Give me your baby, Jake, as soon as you can."

"Oh, Ena." His hands caught her by the waist and lifted her onto the bed. "How about tonight, sweet Ena? Is tonight too soon?"

She ran her hands through his thick hair. "Not soon enough."

He yanked his sweater over his head and tossed it to the floor.

Not touching him—even for those few seconds—was painful.

Rowena reached for his chest as soon as it was bared. When her fingers made contact with his skin, she sighed and closed her eyes to savor the connection. Until...

His fingers began to undo the buttons of her blouse.

Alarms blared through her head. She tried to ignore them and thought she was successful until he drew back.

He kissed her forehead. "What's wrong, sweetheart? Second thoughts?"

"No. Yes. I..." She tried to pull his mouth back to hers. "Please, let's just get this over with."

He wouldn't budge. "Get it over with? Sweetheart, if I have my way, this won't be over for hours, maybe days."

"Oh, Jake." She buried her face in his neck, and in a small voice said, "I have something else to tell you."

"Look at me."

She tried to pull back. "I can't."

"Rowena…"

When he used her full name she knew he was serious. So she forced herself to look at him.

"I understand. You're not a virgin. After all, you're twenty-six. I don't expect…" He trailed off when she shook her head. "That's not it?"

"That's it, but you're wrong. I *am* a virgin."

He went so still, she knew he was horrified.

"I'm sorry! I just couldn't be this intimate with any of them, not after what Heinrich did to me. And—"

"Wait a minute." Jake wrapped his big hands around her face. "What do you mean you couldn't do it with any of them? Gossip around the palace has it that you're practically a…"

"Go ahead and say it. A slut. I know. That's another reason I wouldn't sleep with any of them. To prove everybody wrong."

Jake grinned, then started chuckling. Soon he threw his head back in full-scale laughter.

He didn't stop until she started thumping his chest. "What's wrong with you? This isn't funny."

He wiped tears of laughter from his eyes. "Oh, but it is, my little virgin slut. Only you could pull off something this ridiculous so magnificently."

She didn't know whether to be complimented or outraged. Narrowing her eyes, she once again dug her fingers into the hair on his chest, but this time she wasn't quite so gentle. "Virgin slut, am I?"

He gasped softly at the pleasure/pain, and his hard muscles

quivered beneath her hands. "Tell me something. How can you have never had sex, yet still be so sexy?"

Smiling into blue eyes smoldering once again, she tenderly soothed the skin she'd just abused. "I've been saving up all my fantasies…for you."

If his gaze had been burning before, now it burst into flames. "Like a princess in a fairy tale."

She shook her head. "Fairy tales never go this far."

She tugged gently at the silken hair wrapped around her fingers and pulled him closer.

He came willingly, and she rewarded him by placing a kiss in the concave curve of his chest. "This is real. No sword. No white steed. No dragon. No one needs rescuing tonight. There's just you…and me…and love."

He held her face in his strong, pleasure-giving hands. The way his gaze locked into hers, the awe on his features, made her feel precious and sexy and as far from frigid as a woman could get.

He slowly lowered his head and kissed her tenderly, all the while easing her back onto the bed.

Stretched out together, he arched her into him. She gasped softly at the pleasure of touching him from her lips to her toes.

"Don't worry, sweet Ena," he whispered against her ear. "I'll be as gentle as I can. We'll take all night, if we have to." He chuckled. "Hell, we'll take all night, whether we have to or not."

His hot breath mixed with humor made her love him even more.

She wrapped her arms tightly around him. "So it doesn't bother you?"

"Why would it bother me having a wife who has never been with another man?" He kissed her nose. "No, my love. It makes me feel very special."

She caught her breath. "What did you call me?"

"My love."

She searched his face. "Am I?"

Finally, his face was serious, though he still smiled. "Yes, sweet Ena, you are. I love you."

"You do? How? Why? I thought it wasn't possible."

He shook his head. "I was being stupid. I believed that if I never fell in love again, I'd never be hurt. So I was determined not to give my heart away." He kissed her. "But you stole it when I wasn't looking."

She frowned. "I didn't mean to steal it. In fact, I don't want your heart if you're not giving it to me freely."

He kissed her frown away. "I am. My heart is yours. Keep it safe for me. Lock it up tight."

"No, my love, I'll never lock it away. I'll keep it on a chain around my neck, so I can feel it there every minute of the day, so I can kiss it whenever I need to feel you near."

"Oh, my sweet, sweet heart." His loving eyes searched her face in wonder. "What did I ever do to deserve you loving me? Whatever it was, it must've been pretty damn wonderful."

"All you did, and all you ever need to do, is be you. Just you. That's all I want. Not your money. Not jewels or houses or cars. Just you. Always."

He smiled tenderly. "I know one thing I can give you."

"What?"

"Our baby."

Her face melted into a smile. "All a baby is, my love, is a part of you. The most priceless part. But now that you mention it…weren't we going to get started on making one?"

With a growl, he rolled on top of her. He ravished her mouth until she felt as if she were bursting into flames.

She was so hot, she tore her own clothes off. Then his.

Then Jake slowed things down considerably. He started at her toes and kissed, licked, sucked and gently bit every centimeter of her body. Every centimeter—including all the intimate places no man had ever touched.

Not only did she allow it, she begged him to stop with one breath, then pleaded with him never to stop with the next.

She reached heights of pleasure she'd never known, flying into the clouds. Then she fell back to earth, into his arms, only to have him start all over again.

Hours later, just as he was poised to enter her throbbing body for the first time, he held back. "Tell me."

Burning for him, driven nearly insane with desire, she bucked against him, trying to force him onmy. "Please, Jake. I want you. I need you. NowNowNowNowNow."

He shook his head. "You know what I want to hear."

"I love you!" she cried.

"Yes." He slid in until he felt the proof of her innocence. Smiling with pure male satisfaction, he demanded, "Again."

"I love you. I love you. I love you…"

He made her say it a thousand times before he made her his and they flew into the clouds…together.

"Daddy!"

Jake bolted upright in bed at the panic in Sammy's voice. His bedroom door flew open. "Daddy! Ena's gone!"

Feeling movement beside him, Jake remembered the night's activities. He couldn't suppress a grin as he tossed the sheet over his wife, who, he knew for a fact, was as naked as he was.

Tears streamed down his son's indignant face. "It not funny, Daddy. Where is she?"

"She… umm…" How much did a dad tell a two-year-old about his love life?

Rowena's sleepy voice decided for him. "I'm here, Sammy."

Sammy sniffed. "Ena?"

She raised up enough to rest her chin on Jake's chest. "It's me."

Sammy sniffed even more. "You...You not in your room. I looked."

Jake waved him over. "Come on up, son."

Sammy ran over, and Jake lifted him up.

The boy cocked his head. "You sleep in here, Ena?"

Settling back against the covers, Jake straddled Sammy across his stomach.

Rowena exchanged a secret smile with Jake. He'd never realized how good this kind of intimacy could feel.

"Yes, Sammy. I slept in here."

Sammy rubbed his entire arm across his nose with a residual sniff. "Why?"

Jake lifted a brow at Rowena, who delighted him with a glowing, knowing smile.

"That's what mommies and daddies do, Sammy," Jake answered.

"Why?"

Rowena grinned. "Yes, Daddy, why?"

"Because they love each other."

Sammy cocked his head the other way. "You love me, don't you, Daddy?"

Jake knew what was coming. "Yes, Sammy. I love you very much."

"Can I sleep with you, too?" Sammy's best two-year-old logic.

Damn. What did he say to that?

Rowena must've sensed his dilemma because she chuckled as sat up in bed, stiffly. She slipped one arm around his shoulders and placed her other hand on Sammy's knee. "No, Sammy. You go to sleep too early. We'd disturb you when we came to bed."

"Oh."

Her answer was so perfect, Jake leaned down and rewarded her with a kiss. "You're sore, aren't you?"

She lifted a bare shoulder. "A little."

He nodded. "We'll wait a of couple days."

"No, Jake, I—"

"For what?" Sammy asked.

Jake laughed and tossed his son in the air. "Questions, questions, questions. How can a dad answer so many questions on an empty stomach?"

Sammy squealed in delight, then grinned up at Rowena when he landed flat on Jake's stomach. "Me hungry, too."

She grinned. "All right. I get the message. What do my hungry men want for breakfast?"

Jake frowned as he realized what he'd just done, all for the sake of distracting Sammy. "You don't have to cook for—"

"Oh, yes, I do." She pinched his shoulder at a place Sammy couldn't see. "You're my family, and I love you both. Now what do you want?"

"Are waffles too much trouble?" he asked.

"Booberry!"

"No, booberry waffles are not too much trouble." She chuckled and started to rise from the bed. As soon as she began to peel back the covers, she stopped. "Oh. Ummm, Sammy? Would you please run downstairs and see if we have milk in the icebox?"

"'Kay." Sammy was off the bed and out of the room before they could blink.

Jake captured Rowena before she could make it off the bed. He threw her on her back and hovered over her. "Think we have him fooled?"

She smiled and ran her fingers through his hair. "For a few more years, maybe. But as smart as he is, he'll catch on quick."

"Damn these high IQ genes." Jake's smile softened as he

searched her face and her full, round breasts now bared to him. "You're so beautiful. How did you last twenty-six years in a palace without some handsome, charming, rich statesman talking you into his bed?"

Her nails scratched over the night's growth of his beard. "I was waiting for my real prince to come along."

He dipped low enough to kiss her. "I love you, Princess Rowena."

Her eyes narrowed. "And I love you, *Prince* Jake."

He wrinkled his nose. "What do you say we stick with Mr. and Mrs. Stanbury?"

"I say it's not the best idea you've had all night." She slipped her arms around his neck and pulled his lips to hers. "But it's among the top twenty."

He growled as he kissed her deeply, and molded his hand around her breast. They lost themselves in each other until...

"Daddy! Mommy!" Sammy's footsteps pounded up the stairs.

Jake cursed, but Rowena gasped.

"What is it?" Jake asked.

Her smile was teary, but brilliant. "Sammy just called me Mommy for the first time. At least it's the first time since I've been his mommy."

Jake laid a hand across her stomach and kissed her. "Get used to it, my love. You're going to hear that word the rest of your life."

Chapter Twelve

Rowena's frown slowly turned into a smile as she realized what the two statements lying before her meant. Both were from a trust fund set up for Sammy by Annette's parents. But something wasn't right.

The statement faxed to her this morning showed an amount three-quarters less than that she'd found in Jake's divorce papers from nearly two years earlier.

The account should have grown, not diminished, especially since Annette's parents were still depositing a healthy amount into the account every month.

No one but Jake was authorized to take money out of the trust fund. But someone *was* withdrawing money, and doing so had caused costly penalties.

Rowena knew Jake wasn't taking the money. It had to be Annette.

How Sammy's biological mother had gained access to the account, Rowena didn't know. But not only was it illegal— especially since Annette didn't have custody of Sammy—it proved she wasn't a fit mother. She was stealing from her own son.

Rowena leaned back in the tufted chair with a smile. Now all she had to do was let the judge residing over the case in Virginia know about the theft. Surely he would dismiss Annette's claim.

Or better yet, she'd have Isabel call the judge. Isabel wasn't related to any of the litigants. Plus, she'd been a princess much longer than Rowena had and was a world-reknowned celebrity. Her word would have more clout.

Two days later, Isabel drew Rowena into an alcove. A family dinner was about to begin, but they were the first to arrive. "I had a call from Judge Ewing just as I was leaving my office."

Judge Ewing was the Virginia judge who'd resided over Annette's custody challenge and had issued the order of extradition.

Rowena grabbed Isabel's hands in excitement. "And...?"

"He said he'd talked to Annette's and Jake's lawyers this morning. He's dismissed Annette's custody suit and has rescinded the order of extradition."

"Sammy's safe." Rowena leaned against the wall curving into a thickly glassed window. "Thank God."

Isabel smiled proudly. "God had a lot of help on this one. I never dreamed you were so resourceful. I wasted your talents as a lady-in-waiting. We should've had you in intelligence."

Rowena dismissed her comment. "You can learn a lot about a subject you have a vested interest in. Especially if you...bend the truth a little."

"You had to in order to get access to certain papers. Especially the information on Sammy's trust fund. That's what convinced Judge Ewing. Besides, you *are* Mrs. Stanbury."

"Yes, but not the one they thought was requesting the infor—"

Suddenly Isabel stiffened and her head turned sharply toward the curtain hiding them from the room.

"What is it?" Rowena asked.

"I saw the curtain move, but it's probably just a breeze." Isabel smiled ruefully.

Rowena smiled. "Anyway, Jake is going to be ecstatic about the ruling."

"Well, don't just stand there, find him and tell him."

Rowena shook her head. "I'll let his lawyers call him. He'd want to know how I got the information, and I'd rather not go into that right now."

"Spying again, were you?" Isabel's eyes gleamed with amusement.

But Rowena knew Jake would not be amused. "Not spying, exactly. Just gathering a little information."

Isabel laughed. "Semantics. Well, call it what you like. I still think we could've used you in intelligence."

Intent on getting to Rowena so he could tell her about the call he'd just received from his lawyer, Jake scowled at Luke when he grabbed his arm and pulled him aside.

"What is it?" Jake demanded. "I haven't seen my wife all day."

Luke's smile was nasty. "Still infatuated with the little woman, are you? Maybe not for long."

"What the hell is that supposed to mean? I'm in a hurry, so—"

"I mean your darling little Rowena is not the angel you think she is."

Jake stiffened. "I don't have time for your insults. Go find an insect to torture. That was your favorite occupation when we were young, wasn't it? Or have you graduated to reptiles?"

Luke's eyes narrowed with hate, though his lips still

curved in a facsimile of a smile. "Your loving wife is spying on you."

Jake's fist ached to bash the smirk off his face. He'd wanted to get reacquainted with his brother for Sammy's sake. Now, for Sammy's sake, he wanted to keep Luke the hell away from his son. There were things more important than blood. Rowena had taught him that. "I know she *was,* but she no longer believes I had anything to do with the king's disappearance."

"No longer, as in the last five minutes? Because that's when I heard your wife talking to Princess Isabel."

"They talk all the time."

"About papers your wife requested under false pretenses? Two days ago?"

Jake's heart stuttered, then rallied. "I don't believe you."

"Your ex-wife's custody suit has been dismissed. Apparently just this morning. How would I know that, unless I heard them talking about it? Have you told your wife about it?"

Jake didn't reply. He couldn't. His throat had suddenly frozen shut. He hadn't had time to tell Rowena. He'd just received the news himself.

"No, you didn't," Luke continued smugly. "Princess Isabel told her. I overheard Isabel say she'd just received a call from a Judge Ewing. The name sound familiar?"

Judge Ewing was the one presiding over Annette's suit. There was no way Luke could know that, unless what he said was true.

Luke talked on, giving more details about the conversation between Isabel and Rowena, but Jake barely heard him. The walls of the palace were closing in, and he felt the weight of each stone as it struck his heart…bashing it to pieces.

"Fine, don't believe me," Luke said with obvious disgust.

He thought his torture hadn't worked. Jake's poker face had come through when he'd needed it most. Thank God.

"But if I were you, brother, I'd make a few phone calls before I trusted my wife another second. Virginia is, what, five hours behind us? Six? The bank holding the trust fund will be open for a while. You might even be able to get Judge Ewing on the phone."

Jake didn't reply.

A bell jingled faintly from the formal dining room just down the hall, announcing dinner.

As always, Luke lost interest when his torture didn't work. He turned toward the dining room.

Jake walked in the opposite direction.

Several hours later, Jake stared out the window of the cottage's library, but he was blind to the high waves roiling across the dark, cold North Sea. Blind to everything except his pain.

He'd left the palace and come home to this ancient, dismal house. The house that had, for a few short weeks, been filled with sunshine. False sunshine.

He'd spent the last two hours on the phone talking to the bank and Judge Ewing, only to discover that every word his brother said was true. And more besides. He'd found a file in the desk containing a copy of every document pertaining to his finances, from his divorce papers on.

Rowena now knew his worth down to the last penny.

This woman who'd made him believe she didn't care for his money, didn't care for his title, didn't care for anything except him had betrayed him…as surely as Annette had betrayed him. Not with her body…but with his heart.

This time the betrayal struck deeper. With Annette, he'd seen it coming. Rowena had struck when he wasn't looking, wasn't prepared.

The wound she'd inflicted was deeper. It went all the way to his soul, destroying everything along the way.

He felt hollow, empty, devoid of everything…except the

pain. It was an effort even to breathe. The only reason he made the effort was for Sammy.

What was he going to tell his son? That the woman he'd come to love, come to trust would never leave him, was a lying, heartless—

He stiffened as he heard the front door open.

"Jake?" Rowena called.

She sounded cheerful, with just enough concern thrown in to make him almost believe she loved him.

God, she was good.

Lady-in-waiting, indeed. She was probably the top female agent in intelligence. Edenbourg's version of Mata Hari.

"Are you home?" This time her call came from the parlor.

Seconds later, the door opened behind him. He didn't turn.

"There you are. Why are you standing in the dark?" Her soft tread crossed the carpet. "They told me in the palace nursery that you picked up Sammy before dinner even started. What's wrong? Are you ill?"

Her arms wrapped around his waist from behind. "Why didn't you tell me?"

Damn. Her arms felt warm and loving and safe.

How was that possible…now?

"You're so good at gathering information on your own, I thought you'd know by the time you'd finished the soup course."

She went still. "What are you talking about? Are you sick?"

Sick at heart.

Or he would be, if he still had one.

"No, I'm not sick."

"Then what's wrong?" She reached behind her and switched on a lamp, then tugged on his arm to make him face her.

He let her bring him around, and was glad of the light. He wanted to see her expression.

"Please tell me what's going on." She seemed so sincere.

"Why don't we start with you telling me what's *been* going on? Oh, say, from the moment you moved into this house."

Guilt washed across her face, leaving it pale. She even faltered back a step, as if he'd struck her with more than words. "I...I don't understand. You know why I moved in, and you know everything that's happened since."

He supposed he should be encouraged that she cared enough to feel guilty. Or was it just another of her manipulations?

"You moved in to spy on me."

"Yes." She swallowed visibly. "We've already been through that."

"That's what I thought. However, I seem to recall you agreeing to work with me. Didn't you?"

"Yes." Her voice was small.

Four stiff strides took him to the desk. He picked up a thick folder. "So what is this?"

Rowena wrapped her arms around her waist, trying to keep her plummeting heart from falling to her feet. The folder he held was the one she'd used for the papers she'd received during the past week, the papers that had led to the evidence implicating Annette. "Where did you find that?"

He gave her a pitying look. "Exactly where you left it. At the bottom of all my papers. Very clever. I haven't looked through those papers since I've been here, though I know you have. I only brought them to keep them safe from Annette."

"She has the key to your apartment?"

Rowena knew the question was irrelevant, but she had to gain time some way. Time to think of a way to convince her husband that she'd been working for him, not against him.

The problem was—she was guilty as charged. She'd agreed to tell him what she knew about the investigation on the king, and she hadn't. The fact that the information she'd been gathering to stave off Annette's threat didn't have anything to do with the king wouldn't matter to Jake.

She'd delved deep into his personal affairs, and he assumed she'd done it to discover his guilt.

But beyond that was the fact that she'd told him she would tell him everything, and she hadn't. In fact, she'd lied. He'd asked several times if she knew anything more, and she told him there was no new information in the investigation.

Which, technically, was true. What Isabel had found in his apartment was not considered evidence.

But the technicality was small comfort now. He'd trusted her, and she'd betrayed him.

But he loved her, didn't he? Surely he would understand it was just blind stupidity. Just her not understanding the deeper implications of her actions. Surely he would listen to her.

"No, she doesn't have a key. But she's a beautiful woman who can be very charming when she wants something. I wasn't going to chance her flirting her way past the doorman and into my place via the new super." He dropped the papers with a splat. "But we're not talking about Annette. We're talking about my *new* ex-wife."

Rowena took an involuntary step toward him. "Jake, no. You don't understand."

"Then please enlighten me."

She waved a hand at the file. "I did all that for you. For us. For Sammy."

"For Edenbourg, you mean."

His voice was cold, blowing an icy blast across the desk. "No, Jake, please—"

"I have to give you credit. You had me convinced you loved me."

Hot tears burned her eyes. "Please listen to me, Jake. This wasn't part of the original investigation. It has nothing whatsoever to do with the king. It was stupid female jealousy. When you told me you couldn't love me, I began learning all I could about Annette. I thought maybe if I discovered exactly what she did, I could make it up to you, I could heal your heart. When I compared her pattern of spending with her income, it just grew from there. I finally traced down the withdrawals she was making from Sammy's trust fund. By the time I got to the point where I had useful information, if I'd told you I would've had to confess that I'd been spying on you. I knew you'd act just the way you're acting."

"What you're saying is that you knew how I felt, yet did it anyway."

She tried to swallow the bile rising in her throat. He was right. Utterly, absolutely right. She had no defense. Still, she had to try.

"I'm the one who found the information that stopped Annette's suit. Where is the harm in that?"

"I guess I should thank you for all the work you did, but it's precisely that work that damns you. How can I trust a wife who digs into my affairs, who lies to get personal records and who never tells me what she's doing? If you'd asked, I would've provided you with all this information. Gladly. We could've worked on this…together."

"Jake…"

"You said it yourself, Rowena. Marriage is sharing. What did you share with me? Nothing but lies."

Damned by her own words.

Rowena could barely see him through her tears. It was as if her whole world was melting into the sea.

Jake was right. She said one thing and did another. She was a dishonorable, untrustworthy liar. How could he possibly love her? How could anyone?

"I shared my love with you, Jake. That much is true."

"Save it for someone who believes you."

There was nothing else to say. She turned toward the door, so numb she could barely tell her feet were moving. "I'll say goodbye to Sammy and then—"

"No. I don't want you seeing Sammy again."

She spun to face him. "Jake, please. Sammy loves me. I love him." Her voice broke on a sob, and tears escaped down her cheeks. "You can't just take him away from me."

"He's my son, Rowena. Not yours."

She felt his words like physical blows, pummeling her heart. What could she say to convince him? What could she say to make him believe she loved him?

Nothing. What she'd done was unforgivable, except by someone who loved her. Which Jake obviously didn't. If he wouldn't believe her, what hope did she have?

None.

"I'll pack my—"

"Go now. I'll have Mrs. Hanson pack your things tomorrow, and arrange to have them sent to the palace."

She didn't say anything more. She couldn't.

She turned and moved from the room slowly, concentrating on placing one foot in front of the other, feeling as if she were the rightful occupant of the Dowager Cottage— hopeless, forgotten, freezing cold.

For one brief, beautiful moment, she'd glimpsed happily ever after. But that's all it was—a shadow in the corner of her eye, vanishing when she got too close.

It was a lesson she was never going to forget.

Chapter Thirteen

"So the maids were right. You're back."

Rowena didn't start, didn't even blink at Isabel's comment directly behind her, though she hadn't heard the princess enter the room. All Rowena's defenses were being used at the moment, trying to rebuild her heart.

They weren't working.

Isabel stepped around the chaise and sat by Rowena's knees, but didn't face her. The princess turned toward the view Rowena had been staring at all night…the sea.

"Since you're still wearing the dress you wore to dinner, I'm guessing you haven't been to bed."

"Go away."

Isabel glanced over her shoulder with an arch smile that was somehow sympathetic at the same time. "You know me better than that."

Unfortunately, Rowena did. Isabel had the tenacity and patience of a turtle on a mile-long hike.

"You look like hell," Isabel added before she turned back around. "That's the curse of being a redhead. Everyone knows when you've been crying."

"Thank you."

"You're welcome."

Several minutes of silence later, Isabel sighed. "Might as well make it easy on yourself. You know I'll get it out of you eventually."

"What's there to say? Jake threw me out."

"Just like that."

"Just like that."

"For no reason at all."

"He had plenty of reasons. Good reasons. The biggest, of course, being that I betrayed him."

That brought Isabel's whole body around. "Rowena! You've only been married two weeks. I know you've dated more than one man at a time in the past, but I never believed you—"

"Not with another man. By gathering information behind his back. By spying on him."

Isabel paled. "Oh God, Rowena, forgive me. I never meant for something like this to happen when we talked about you being his nanny. This is all my fault. I have to—"

"No, Isabel." Rowena reached for her friend's hand. It was the most she'd moved for over twelve hours, and she was so stiff that moving hurt. "It's not your fault. I didn't tell you this, but Jake caught me going through his papers before you even went to New York. He could've kicked me out then. Instead, he asked if we could work together. I agreed, and the whole time I had the key in my pocket that you used to search his apartment. He still doesn't know about that. At least, he didn't mention it."

"Then why did he tell you to leave?"

"Because I gathered information on Annette. By necessity, I had to obtain financial information on Jake as well. He found the files, and thinks we still consider him a suspect, that I believe he's guilty."

"Doesn't he realize what you did for him? If it hadn't been for you doing all that work, he'd still be fighting his ex-wife's suit. What did he say when you pointed that out?"

Rowena leaned back against the chaise, exhausted by the effort it took to lean forward. "He thanked me, but said it doesn't matter. He can't trust a wife who sneaks around behind his back, gathering information he would've given her had she just asked. You can't blame him."

Isabel frowned. "Oh, yes I can. What you did—no matter how you did it—let him out from between the rock and the hard place he'd been squirming in. He should be grateful his wife is so enterprising."

Rowena shook her head. "Jake's right. I continued spying on him after I agreed we'd work together. That makes me as guilty as he thinks I am."

"But you did it for him."

"He's a lawyer, Isabel. Everything is black and white to him. Betrayal is betrayal."

Isabel's green eyes narrowed. "So you're just going to sit here on your rumpus, crying at the sea."

Rowena lifted her shoulder.

"The sea doesn't care whether you're crying or not, Rowena. It won't lift a single wave to help you. Only you can get what you want."

"How can I have what I want when my marriage is over? Jake wouldn't even let me pack my things. He told me I couldn't..." Her voice cracked. "Told me I couldn't see Sammy again. Ever."

"You hurt him. He was lashing out in pain. But he's had all night to think about it. I'll bet he's as miserable as you. He loves you, Rowena."

"Loved me, you mean."

Isabel shook her head. "Love like I've seen on his face doesn't vanish overnight."

"He probably won't even let me in the house."

"You have a key."

"He won't listen to me."

"Make him listen. Sit in the middle of his bed until he can't do anything but listen."

Damn Isabel for using logic. She was building hope, and Rowena knew there was none. "You don't know Jake like I do."

"Do you still love him, Rowena?"

"Of course I do. I always will, no matter what he does."

"Then isn't he worth fighting for? Isn't your marriage? If not, then your love wasn't strong enough to begin with."

Rowena curled her legs up under her. "I do love him. You just don't understand."

Isabel waved a dismissing hand. "Tell it to the seagulls, maybe they will."

Rowena's fists struck the arms of the chaise. "Why are you being so mean?"

"I never knew you to be a coward, Rowena." Isabel stood. "I tell you one thing. If I had a man who looked at me the way Jake looks at you, I wouldn't sit here crying. I'd hang on to him and wouldn't let go until the earth spun off its axis. Until all the stars melted together. Until the universe went up in flames. Until—"

"I get it."

Isabel sighed, then leaned down and placed a kiss on Rowena's forehead. "Wash your face before you go. You look like hell."

"What makes you think I'm going anywhere?"

"I have faith in your good sense."

Rowena refused to watch her friend leave the room.

Damn Isabel. Rowena had never won an argument with her.

If she couldn't stand up to Isabel, how could she stand up to Jake?

Isn't he worth fighting for? If not, then your love wasn't strong enough to begin with.

Was her love strong enough? Strong enough to try again? Strong enough to take rejection after rejection? Because that could happen, knowing Jake. Weeks, months, maybe even years of rebuffs.

Seeing the hurt and hatred in his eyes last night was the most painful experience she'd ever had. Far worse than facing all the gossips who'd believed Heinrich's lies. Worse, even, than losing her mother.

At least she'd known her mother was no longer in pain. She couldn't say the same for Jake.

Jake…who believed in happily ever after so strongly, he'd made her believe in it again.

What did he think of it now? Had she destroyed his faith in his ability to create it for Sammy, and for himself?

That possibility, more than anything, convinced her she couldn't sit crying any longer. She had to find Jake and make him understand.

Because her love was strong enough. Strong enough to keep believing in happily ever after.

Because love *was* happily ever after.

Jake stayed behind in the conference room while everyone else filed out for a mid-morning break. He didn't need to stretch his legs. It took all his energy to maintain a calm demeanor.

The main person he didn't want knowing what had happened was Luke. Jake didn't want to give his brother the satisfaction of knowing he'd destroyed Jake's happiness.

Although, he supposed, he should thank his brother for showing him the kind of woman he'd married.

And he might, if only he could convince himself Rowena was the seductress he'd believed last night.

After she'd left, he went back over the documents in the

file which he'd only scanned earlier. The second time he'd clearly seen the path she'd taken to the correct conclusions she'd drawn. Every document she'd requested led her to more information about Annette, not him.

Her claim to have been investigating Annette seemed to be true.

So…what about her other claims? Specifically, her claim to love him?

He wanted to believe in her love more than he wanted to believe the sun would rise the next morning.

But he was afraid to. Where women were concerned, he'd already proven he didn't have the same ability to read people as he did in business relationships.

Where women were concerned, he was batting zero for two. One more strike and he was out for good. Giving Rowena another chance could prove to be his last strike.

Suddenly the silence in the conference room was shattered by the ringing of the phone on the credenza behind the head chair.

Jake let it ring several times. When no one came to answer it, he rose and lifted the receiver. Having no idea how to answer, he merely said, "Hello?"

"Hello, sir? I have a caller who claims to have information about King Michael, and I thought I should put the call through."

"Yes. Please do." He craned to see if there was anyone close enough to take the call. There wasn't.

A few clicks later, a muffled voice asked, "Is this the prince?"

Jake hesitated. If he said no, this person—it sounded like a woman, but he wasn't sure—might hang up and the information would be lost. Besides, everyone kept telling him he was a prince. "Yes. Can I help you?

"Keep looking. The king is still alive."

"Where is he? Who is this?"

"A friend. I have to go. King Michael is safe…for the moment."

"Where is he? Can you at least give me a clue?"

There was no answer but the dial tone.

Jake depressed the switch and connected with the operator.

"Yes sir?"

"Tell me you have caller ID."

"Yes, sir. But it will be a moment before we can trace down the exact location of the number. All I can tell you now is that the call was made from Edenbourg."

"Good. Let me know when you have the information."

"Yes, sir."

Jake replaced the receiver. He had to tell someone. Now. But who?

Rowena.

Jake shook his head.

Why would she be the first person to pop into his mind? The prince and his ministers were out on the terrace. At least, that's where they'd headed. And except for her task of spying on him, Rowena had nothing to do with the investigation.

Even so, he knew he'd take the information to his wife. She was the only person he trusted not to jump to the conclusion that the reason he knew the king was alive was because he'd kidnapped him.

The only person he trusted.

His attention caught on those words.

They were true. He trusted her. He believed in her. He loved her.

The realization felt good, felt right, felt inevitable. Yet it was frightening at the same time. Because he didn't know what to do now.

He certainly hadn't acted as if he loved or believed or trusted her. Not in the past eighteen hours.

He'd had his reasons. Last night he was in anguish thinking he'd been betrayed...again.

But Rowena hadn't betrayed him. She'd helped him.

Yes, she'd been wrong not to tell him what she was doing and why she was doing it, but she'd admitted she shouldn't have gone behind his back. Her reasons were that her original motive had changed once she delved into Annette's spending habits.

Reasons. Reasons. They were just excuses for them to protect themselves. He was as bad as she was. And there was no excuse for that. Not if he loved her.

The information she'd gathered had saved him months, perhaps even years of nasty custody battles—with Sammy getting old enough to remember them.

Didn't that prove his sweet Rowena had been working for him, not against him?

She did love him.

No woman had ever worked so hard for him, for something he wanted as much as he wanted his son. She was the only woman who'd ever delved into his psyche, who cared to know Jake the man.

He had to go to her. He had to confess his stupidity and beg her forgiveness. Beg her to love him forever. Together, they could create happily ever...

Damn.

He'd forgotten.

His offense was far worse than he thought.

One reason Rowena loved him was because he'd renewed her faith in happily ever after. Now look what he'd done. He'd proved her worst fear—that it doesn't exist.

He had to find her—now. What's more, he had to give her all of his heart. He'd been keeping part of it safe, hidden away from her...in case something like this happened.

But that was cheating. Happily ever after demanded everything. All of his effort. All of his soul. All of his heart.

He had to find her. Each moment he hesitated was a moment lost, a moment for her to dwell on how much he'd hurt her.

If he were very, very lucky, she might listen to him.

If he were the luckiest man on earth, she might believe him.

He turned to leave when the phone rang again. He picked it up. "Yes?"

"Sir, the call was made from the pay phone at the southwest corner of the block containing the art museum. No one was there when the police arrived."

"Thank you."

"You're welcome, sir."

Jake replaced the receiver with a smile. At least he had a way to get his foot in Rowena's door.

After she let him in, it was up to his lips—and his heart—to convince her to let him stay.

Just as Jake's knuckles struck the wood of Rowena's door, it opened.

He drew back in surprise, and so did she when she saw him.

"Jake!" She took a hesitant step forward, her face lighting up. Then her defenses kicked in. She stopped and dropped her gaze to his chest. "I was just coming to find you."

"You were?" He reached out and lifted her chin. "You've been crying."

Her hands touched her cheeks. "I thought I'd splashed enough cold water on my eyes so you couldn't tell."

"Damn. You're so beautiful."

His whispered words made her eyes widen. "I am? Oh, Jake, I... What are you doing here?"

"I..." He was torn between saving his marriage and saving the king. The lawyer in him won. He'd still be here after Rowena delivered the information to whoever needed it.

Besides, how she delivered the information—and to whom—would tell him a lot about the way she felt.

"I was alone in the conference room when a call came in about the king."

She blinked, then pulled him into her room and closed the door. "What did they say?"

"They said that the king is alive, and we should keep looking. I asked the caller who they were, how they knew, if they would please give us a hint where the king was, but that's all they would say. That Uncle Michael is safe, for now."

She spun toward the door. "We have to tell the family."

He grabbed her arm to stop her. "If you tell them I intercepted the call, they'll think there wasn't a call at all. They'll think I know he's alive because I kidnapped him and am holding him for some nefarious purpose of my own. This would be just one more piece of circumstantial evidence laid on the pyre at my feet."

"You came to me first?" When he nodded, her golden hazel eyes shone with wonder. "You knew I wouldn't think that."

He nodded.

Her smile came from every part of her body. "You trust me."

He slipped an arm around her waist. "With all my heart."

"Oh, Jake." She threw her arms around his neck. "Will you please, *please* kiss me? It's been forever."

He did, and it was the most beautiful, the most passionate, the most loving kiss he'd ever had. He never wanted to let go.

But finally, he had to let her breathe.

He rested his forehead against hers. "As much as I want to continue this, shouldn't we tell someone about the call?"

"Yes." She drew back with a rueful smile. "I'm glad one of us has some sense."

He pushed away a strand of hair caught on her cheek. "If you think the information about the phone call can wait..."

She shook her head regretfully. "This is the biggest development they've had since the king disappeared. It proves that he's still alive. I'll ring Isabel and ask her to call the family together. That way you can tell them all at the same time."

He frowned. "You want me to tell them? They'll still think—"

"No, they won't." She smiled. "Trust me. All right?"

He'd thought he'd be testing her love, now he found his tested in return. "All right. I will."

She stood on tiptoe and kissed him. "Thank you."

Fifteen minutes later, Jake walked into another conference room, hand-in-hand with Rowena. The royal family were already seated, along with the top officers of the royal security, including Lieutenant Commander Adam Sinclair of the Edenbourg navy, who'd been called in by Isabel. He'd apparently been delayed by a mission abroad or he would've been involved from the beginning.

Rowena introduced Jake's message briefly, then he related, word for word, the entire conversation, plus the follow-up on the location of the call.

The first comment came from the queen, and it was exactly what Jake feared. "How did you happen to be the one to take this call? You're the main suspect, as I recall. How do we know you didn't make this phone call up?"

Jake stiffened. "I'm sure the operator has a log of calls received. If not, there will be a record of the trace."

"You could've hired someone to make the call, to throw suspicion off you."

Jake was sick of being told he was family, then being treated like the black sheep. "I'll tell you—"

Rowena's irate voice cut him off. "How dare you talk to my husband that way?"

He turned to see her facing the queen with her hands on her hips.

"I'm sorry to be rude, Your Majesty, but I'm tired of you—all of you—holding out your hand in friendship to him only to slap him with it. My husband did not kidnap yours. I'm as sure of that as I am that Prince Nicholas didn't do it. And he's a suspect, too, remember. If this is the way you treat your family, I don't care to be a part of it."

Jake had never loved her more. When she finished her tirade, he held out his arms.

She walked straight into them. "I'm sorry, Jake. You trusted me, and I let you down."

He kissed her forehead. "Can we go?"

She nodded but before they could leave, they were stopped by authoritative words.

"Rowena is absolutely correct." Nicholas stood. "Jake proved his loyalty by risking his life to save mine and Rebecca's. I didn't know there was anyone who still considered him a suspect. I'm sorry, Mother, if we didn't make that clear."

The prince faced Jake. "And I apologize to you for not having said something before."

Jake nodded.

"I agree with Nicholas," Isabel said. "Jake saved the life of the heir to the throne. Why would he do that if he wanted the throne for himself? The same incident exonerates Nicholas, as well, in my opinion. He would never have placed Rebecca in such jeopardy."

"If I may speak…"

Nicholas nodded at Lieutenant Commander Adam Sinclair.

"Princess Isabel is right. If Prince Nicholas had staged the aborted kidnapping, he and his cousin would've had to be working together. And we know for a fact the two never met until after the king's disappearance. The prince's whereabouts are too closely monitored for there to be any doubt about that."

"Thank you, Adam." Nicholas turned to his security officers. "Are we clear on this? Don't waste any more time investigating Jake Stanbury. He's no longer a suspect."

The officers nodded. One made a note on his pad.

Nicholas waved at two empty chairs. "Both of you are family now. Please join our discussion."

As they made their way around the table, the prince asked, "Jake, what about Edward and Luke? Should we invite them to sit in, too?"

Jake used pulling out Rowena's chair as an excuse to cover his hesitation. He knew his father didn't have the...organizational skills to successfully pull off a king's kidnapping, but Edward did have the ambition. And Luke had the skills. However, Jake didn't want to voice disloyalty to his immediate family.

"It's all right, Jake," Nicholas urged. "Nothing you say will be repeated outside this room."

Jake gripped the back of his chair. "Can I get by with saying that I see no reason to include them in this discussion?"

"We understand." Nicholas addressed the room at large. "Let's begin. What can we ascertain from this phone call?"

Jake sat, then slipped his hand into Rowena's lap and covered her folded ones. She laced the fingers of one hand through his. They sat that way through several hours of discussion.

Ultimately, the family decided on a bold and somewhat risky move. They would entreat Queen Josephine's favorite nephew—Benjamin Lockhart, who was a ringer for Prince Nicholas—to act as a decoy and allow himself to be kidnapped. If it worked, this should lead them to whoever was behind the king's kidnapping.

The queen was hesitant, preferring not to endanger her

nephew, but she finally agreed since there were few other options. Benjamin was a lieutenant in the Edenbourg navy, after all, and trained to handle difficult situations.

Nicholas didn't like the idea much either, because it required him to go into hiding, an act he considered cowardly. However, he finally agreed it was necessary both to find the king and to protect himself and his family. Being reminded of Rebecca's wound was what convinced him.

As soon as the meeting was over, Jake turned to Rowena. "Can we talk?"

"Please."

"Where?"

She hesitated. "Can we go home?"

He smiled. "As long as 'home' is the Dowager Cottage."

"Yes."

Without releasing her hand, he stood and led her onto the terrace. Suddenly, the walk through the garden seemed far too long. Instead of guiding her down the stairs off the terrace, he pulled her into an alcove.

"What are you—"

He covered her mouth with his.

She only took a second to recover from the surprise and melt into him, whimpering and standing on tiptoe to get closer.

Jake gathered her in, sparking the connection he'd lost and missed so much it was torment.

An eternity had passed since he'd kissed her, held her. It felt as if he had an armful of heaven.

"Let's go home," she whispered as he broke off to rain kisses down her neck. "Please, Jake, please."

Her plea required thought, which broke desire's hold on him enough for sanity to return. At least, enough to let reason rule over passion. "It's best if we don't."

"Jake, you promised."

He kissed her nose. "We'll go home, my love, but first

we need to talk this through. There are things that need to be said before we fall into bed.''

She sucked in a tiny breath. ''Am I?''

He smiled sadly, for giving her doubt. ''Yes, you are my love. At least, if you can forgive me.''

''For what?''

''For not listening to you. For forcing you to leave. For trampling all over your newly found faith in happily ever after. The list of my offenses is so long, I could never get to the end of them.''

''But not too long to forgive.'' She rubbed her hand down his cheek. ''If you can forgive mine.''

His kiss was as soft as a butterfly's. ''What is there to forgive? All you did was search for information that lets us keep our son.''

''I still haven't told you everything. Remember when you asked that we work together? The whole time, I had your apartment key in my pocket. I made a copy of it and Isabel used it to search your apartment in New York.''

He frowned. ''And what did she find?''

''Nothing but some books about the royal family.''

He nodded. ''I needed those when I helped my father a few months ago. He was serving as commerce liaison between Edenbourg and the U.S. and was facing a crisis with an import/export matter. Since he wanted his superiors to think he'd solved the crisis himself, I wasn't allowed to tell anyone I helped him.''

''I knew there was a good explanation.''

''Again, my love, I would've given you the key, if you'd just asked.''

Rowena sighed. ''I'm so sorry, Jake. I knew Isabel wouldn't find anything, but I had to give her the key. I'd already promised, and she was itching to *do* something. At that point they didn't have any leads at all.''

He kissed her temple. ''I guess we both have a little forgiving to do. But that's what marriage is all about. That's what creates happily ever after.''

"So you'll take me back?"

"Are you kidding? I insist. In fact, if you don't come back, I'll come get you…wherever you are, whatever you're doing, whoever you're with.''

She relaxed against him. "And offer me money, no doubt. Or jewelry. Come to think of it, I'm surprised you don't have anything to give me now. Is it just because you didn't have time to shop before you found me?''

He shook his head. "You've taught me that lesson well, my love. Marriage is not a merger, and a wife is not an acquisition. Loving you means I have to give you everything, with no expected return on my capital. But if that's what you want, I'll give it all to you—all my money, all the jewels in the world—as long as you take my heart along with them.''

"Oh, Jake. You're my prince in shining armor. How could I ask for anything more when all I want is you?''

He kissed her, solemnly this time. "Come home with me, my love, and stay forever. You're the only woman who can make my ever after happy.''

Epilogue

"Mommy?"

Rowena smiled as she closed the front door behind her. What a lovely sound to come home to.

"Dat you?"

"Yes, Sammy-Jammy. I'm home."

There was a flash at the door of the parlor, then Sammy appeared from the blur when he finally stopped. "Guess what, Mommy?"

She held out her arms and he ran into them. When she lifted him, he wrapped his legs around her waist and his arms around her neck.

She squeezed him tightly. "I know what."

He pulled back and peered at her, his head cocked to the side. "You do?"

"I know I love you."

He grinned. "I love you, too, Mommy, but that's not what."

"No?" A movement at the parlor door caught her eye and she glanced over to see Jake lounging against the back of the settee.

He seemed perfectly content just to watch them.

She wondered if he knew that the queen's nephew, Benjamin Lockhart, had been kidnapped according to plan, en route to an important engagement. Prince Nicholas—willing to hide to protect his family—had disappeared to a safe place only a few people knew about.

According to the Treatise of Edenbourg, Jake's father, Edward, was now acting king. Luke was next in line, then Jake.

"Mommy?" Sammy's small hands brought her face around to his. "That's not what."

"Then what is what?" It was Sammy's version of Who's On First...one of his favorite games.

"Guess what."

"Okay. Your father has just been appointed the liaison in import/export commerce between Edenbourg and the United States." She meandered toward her husband.

The wry look on Jake's face said he knew, which meant he also knew about the kidnapping. His expression also said he wasn't sure how long the prestigious position would last, since it had been awarded to him by his father, who had no permanent authority.

Sammy's face scrunched up. "Huh?"

Having ascertained what she wanted to know, Rowena brought her attention back to her son. "No? Hmmm. Let's see. You flew to the moon."

Sammy giggled. "No, Mommy. Guess 'gin."

"You went to the library with Daddy."

"Yes, but dat's not what either."

"You got married."

He scrunched his face. "Kiss a girl? Icky icky. No!"

"Daddy doesn't mind kissing a girl." Rowena lifted her lips to Jake's.

He kissed her thoroughly, then grinned down at her. "Icky."

Because her hands were full, she bumped a hip into him. "Icky, huh? I'll remind you that you thought so...later."

"You taste about as icky as a double fudge sundae." Jake captured her hips and pulled her around so he could lean her back against him.

Rowena sighed happily and placed a kiss on Sammy's nose. "See?"

"You're not a girl, Mommy," Sammy informed her matter-of-factly. "You're a mommy."

"You're right, I am. And guess what, Sammy?"

"What, Mommy?"

"I'm glad."

"Guess what, Mommy?"

"Are you going to tell me this time?"

He nodded and grinned at his father. "Me and Daddy bought you a—"

Jake placed a hand over Sammy's mouth. "No, Sammy, it's a surprise. You're not supposed to tell her yet."

"Uh-oh. I forgetted."

"Tell me what?" Rowena demanded.

Jake had discovered in the last few weeks that she lost all her thought processes when he nibbled on her ear. Now he took advantage of the way he'd positioned her by doing it. "Forget it."

She pulled away to keep her wits. "What did you buy?"

"Don't go looking like that, Ena." He threw a sour look at Sammy. "Thanks a lot, son."

Sammy wiggled in Rowena's arms, and she set him down. "Jake..."

Sammy took off upstairs.

"Damn. I have to show you now or you'll think the worst." He stepped around the couch and picked up a small shopping bag from the coffee table.

When he withdrew a velvet box, Rowena's hands went to her hips. "I told you—"

"Oh, hush, Rowena Stanbury. I can buy my wife jewelry if I want." His expression softened, and he held out a hand. "Come here." When she hesitated, he added, "Please, beautiful Ena."

"Compliments won't work either." But she stepped around the settee and slipped her hand into his.

He smiled and drew her with him down onto the settee.

She straightened her skirt, then looked at him. "Well?"

He turned her hand palm up, placed a kiss in the middle of it, then the box. "The first night we made love you said something I'll never forget. I wanted to give you something to remind you of your words, so you'll always remember them, so they'll always be true."

Her brows wrinkled. "Which words?"

"You told me you'll never lock my heart away. You said you'll keep it on a chain around your neck, so you can feel it there every minute of the day, to feel me near." He opened the box on her hand. "Since it would be rather messy—not to mention fatal—to give you my actual heart to wear on a chain, I had to settle for this symbol."

Rowena's breath drew in. An unbelievably perfect ruby sparkled against the white satin lining, perfectly faceted in the shape of a heart. But it was Jake's words that brought tears to her eyes.

She touched the stone. It felt warm, almost as if it had its own pulse.

"Will you wear this, my love, and think of me?"

She met his loving gaze. "Oh, Jake. Yes, of course. I'll wear it with pride, and tell everyone who comments on it what it means. As long as it comes with the real thing."

He kissed her reverently. "Sweet Ena, you've possessed my heart from the first moment I saw you."

He took the ruby from the box and fastened the chain around her neck.

"I love you, Jake."

"I know you do, my love. And my heart is yours. Here." He kissed the ruby, then captured her hand and placed it against his heart. "And here. For as long as either is on the earth."

She touched the ruby lying in the cleft of her throat. "Jewels last for thousands of years. Probably millions, if they're taken care of."

He pulled her onto his lap. "Then take good care of it, sweet Ena."

She wrapped her arms around his neck. "I will, my love. Always...and happily..." she kissed him "...ever..." she kissed him again ...after.

* * * * *

Turn the page for a sneak preview
of the next ROYALLY WED *title*

CODE NAME: PRINCE

Ren and Meagan's story!
By popular author Valerie Parv
On sale in May 2001 in Silhouette Romance...

Chapter One

Ben Lockhart's first waking thought was how much he would like to get his hands on whoever was using a jackhammer inside his head. He opened his eyes then snapped them shut again. Letting the light in was a really bad idea. So was moving.

He made himself lie still and think. As a navy man he wasn't anybody's idea of an angel, but he could usually remember what he'd done to get this hungover, especially when the party was as spectacular as last night's must have been. Yet try as he might, he couldn't recall a single detail.

Then it came back to him. He couldn't remember the party because there hadn't been one. He had been doubling for his cousin, Prince Nicholas Stanbury, acting king of Edenbourg while King Michael was missing and believed kidnapped.

The pounding in Ben's head reminded him painfully that his last memory was of being dragged into a limousine that had infiltrated the royal cavalcade. Falling for the pretense that he was Prince Nicholas, his captors had blindfolded and bound him then injected him with a knockout drug, leaving him to wake up here, wherever here was.

Ben felt a frown start, wishing that his headache *had* been due to over-indulgence. It would have been easier to deal with than the task ahead of him. Now he had to find out who was behind these attacks on the royal family.

Easy enough if you said it quickly, Ben thought, wincing as movement sent a fresh wave of pain surging through his skull. What in the name of Edenbourg had they given him? He opened his eyes more cautiously, hoping he could get a look at his watch and try to work out how long he'd been unconscious, only to find his hands were securely tied to the white wrought-iron bedstead on which he lay. A battered teddy bear sat on the pillow beside his head.

Teddy bear? What sort of kidnappers kept a teddy bear? Ignoring the urge to close his eyes again, he waited until the room stopped spinning then made himself take stock. He was lying on a diminutive bed, his feet overhanging the end by a good six inches, the bed evidently being meant for someone a lot smaller than his six-foot frame.

Beside the bed stood a white-painted dresser. On it sat a stuffed dog, a homemade rag doll and a water glass that made him lick his dry lips, wishing he could reach it. Above the dresser was a multi-paned window hung with dainty floral curtains that matched the frilled coverlet beneath him. On the opposite wall were two doors. One he presumed led to a closet and the other into the rest of the house. Right now, both doors were closed.

Twisting his body to try to see out the window and get an idea of where he was only resulted in making the rope bite deeper into his wrists, adding to his discomfort. He made himself lie still. His captors hadn't gone to this much trouble to let him die of starvation or thirst. Sooner or later somebody was bound to come in and check on him. Until then it made more sense to rest and let the drug work its way out of his system.

He didn't have long to wait.

After what he judged to be about half an hour he saw the china handle on one of the doors begin to turn. He closed his eyes and slowed his breathing with the idea of buying himself a few minutes to assess his captor.

He heard tentative footsteps on the polished wood floor as someone approached the bed, but the first thing that hit him was the scent of roses. It struck him as being as incongruous as the teddy bear. He was so startled that he almost opened his eyes to get a look at the source of the delicious scent teasing his nostrils like a breath of spring.

"I know you're awake."

The soft, musical voice so exactly matched the scent that another shock wave rippled through him, as well as something much more basic. He scolded himself to resist it. Obviously, his captor was a woman, but that didn't mean he had to react like a man. The problem seemed to be convincing his body. This time he did open his eyes, barely remembering to do it slowly to create the impression that he was only now coming around.

What met his eyes was so unexpected that he would have jerked upright if not for the ropes binding him to the bed. Leaning over him was the most beautiful woman he had ever seen. Tall and willowy, she had hair the color of ripe corn scattered with paler highlights, over eyes as blue as a summer sky. He saw that they were clouded now with something—fear? It seemed odd, given that he was the captive.

He reminded himself again that she was one of the kidnappers. Not one of those who had abducted and drugged him. If she had been, he knew he would have noticed her scent even as he was going under. So she hadn't been part of that scene. But she was here and despite the naked fear he read in her eyes, she made no move to untie him.

"How did you know I was awake?" he asked, hearing his voice rasp as an after-effect of his rough treatment.

She heard it too, because she picked up the glass of water

from the dresser and lifted it to his lips. With her free hand, she supported his head so he could drink. Her fingers felt like the caress of velvet against the back of his neck. When some of the water dribbled down his chin, she put the glass down long enough to brush the droplets away with the back of her hand. He felt a strong urge to capture those delicate fingers in his mouth.

What was he thinking? She was the enemy, remember? Probably chosen precisely because his captors expected her golden good looks to soften him up so he'd tell them whatever they needed to know. Well, to perdition with that idea. He'd tell them nothing. Nor would he think of her as an angel, when she was in league with whoever had captured him.

"Your eyelids were moving just the way Molly's do when she wants me to think she's asleep," the woman answered his question.

"And Molly is?"

She hesitated, then said, "My daughter."

Molly must be the child who normally slept in this room, he concluded. At the same time he wondered what kind of woman allowed her child to become involved in criminal activities.

He turned his head to one side and she took the hint, replacing the glass on the dresser. "Who are you?" he demanded.

The haunted look that had disappeared when he asked about Molly returned to her eyes, but he hardened his heart against it. "I can't tell you," she said in a voice barely above a whisper. Who was she afraid might hear her?

"At least tell me your first name." It came to him that he wanted to know as much to satisfy his own curiosity as to help his mission.

Her frightened glance flew to the door then back to him. "Meagan," she said. "You can call me Meagan."

Don't miss the reprisal of
Silhouette Romance's popular miniseries

When
King Michael of
Edenbourg goes
missing,

Royally Wed
The Stanbury Crown

his devoted
family and loyal
subjects make it
their mission to bring
him home safely!

Their search begins March 2001 and
continues through June 2001.

On sale March 2001: **THE EXPECTANT PRINCESS**
by bestselling author **Stella Bagwell** (SR #1504)

On sale April 2001: **THE BLACKSHEEP PRINCE'S BRIDE**
by rising star **Martha Shields** (SR #1510)

On sale May 2001: **CODE NAME: PRINCE**
by popular author **Valerie Parv** (SR #1516)

On sale June 2001: **AN OFFICER AND A PRINCESS**
by award-winning author **Carla Cassidy** (SR #1522)

Available at your favorite retail outlet.

Silhouette®
Where love comes alive™

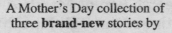

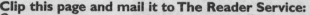

Silhouette
bestselling authors

KASEY MICHAELS

RUTH LANGAN

CAROLYN ZANE

*welcome you to a world
of family, privilege and power
with three brand-new love
stories about America's
most beloved dynasty,
the Coltons*

Brides of Privilege

Available May 2001

Silhouette®
Where love comes alive™

Silhouette® —

where love comes alive—online...

shop eHarlequin

- ❤ Find all the new Silhouette releases at everyday great discounts.
- ❤ Try before you buy! Read an excerpt from the latest Silhouette novels.
- ❤ Write an online review and share your thoughts with others.

reading room

- ❤ Read our Internet exclusive daily and weekly online serials, or vote in our interactive novel.
- ❤ Talk to other readers about your favorite novels in our Reading Groups.
- ❤ Take our Choose-a-Book quiz to find the series that matches you!

authors' alcove

- ❤ Find out interesting tidbits and details about your favorite authors' lives, interests and writing habits.
- ❤ Ever dreamed of being an author? Enter our Writing Round Robin. The Winning Chapter will be published online! Or review our writing guidelines for submitting your novel.

SINTB1R

Beginning in May from

Silhouette Romance™

THE TEXAS BROTHERHOOD

A brand-new series by
PATRICIA THAYER

As boys, the ill-fated birthright left to the Randell
brothers by their father almost tore them apart.
As men, they created a legacy of their own....

Don't miss any of their stories!

CHANCE'S JOY (SR #1518)
On sale May 2001

A CHILD FOR CADE (SR #1524)
On sale June 2001

TRAVIS COMES HOME (SR #1530)
On sale July 2001

Available only from Silhouette Romance
at your favorite retail outlet.

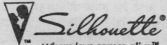

Silhouette®
Where love comes alive™

Visit Silhouette at www.eHarlequin.com   SRTTB